A LOVE LIKE YOU

MEN OF THE MISFIT INN
BOOK 6

KAIT NOLAN

TAKE THE LEAP PUBLISHING

Copyright © 2023 by Kait Nolan

All rights reserved.

A LETTER TO READERS

Dear Reader,

This book features characters from the Deep South. As such, it contains a great deal of colorful, colloquial, and occasionally grammatically incorrect language. This is a deliberate choice on my part as an author to most accurately represent the region where I have lived my entire life. This book also contains swearing and pre-marital sex between the lead couple, as those things are part of the realistic lives of characters of this generation, and of many of my readers.

If any of these things are not your cup of tea, please consider that you may not be the right audience for this book. There are scores of other books out there that are written with you in mind. In fact, I've got a list of some of my favorite authors who write on the sweeter side on my website at https://kaitnolan.com/on-the-sweeter-side/

If you choose to stick with me, I hope you enjoy!

Happy reading!

Kait

ONE

Clipboard in hand, Mick Routledge leaned past the two-foot Christmas tree that perched at one end of the long-scarred counter, the only concession Willie Thompson made in his garage to the upcoming holiday. "I got those brake pads changed out for you and gave the whole car a good once-over. You had a small leak in your radiator hose that could've turned into something bigger, and we had one in stock, so I went ahead and changed that out, as well. Everything else looks good."

Essie Vaughn nodded and plunked her massive purse on the counter. "Thank you, Mick. I don't know what I'd do without you keeping this old car going."

Mick knew it pained the older woman that her late husband was no longer around to keep up with the maintenance himself. As Mr. Vaughn had been one of his favorite teachers back in high school, Mick was happy to do whatever he could to ease the older woman's burdens. "You know I'll keep her going as long as I can."

He accepted her credit card and began ringing up the invoice.

"Big plans after work tonight?" Essie asked.

"Dinner with the Teagues. Erin's making pot roast, and I'm not about to be turning that down."

Essie's eyes brightened. "Oh, I think they were supposed to find out what the sex of the baby is today. Any word?"

"Not a one." He handed the credit card back. "I think they're very much in the planning-to-surprise-everybody-when-Baby-Teague-gets-here camp."

Her face fell a little. "I was hoping to be one of the first in the know."

As dispatcher for the Sheriff's Department, Essie usually was one of the primary gossip hubs in town. Any time she got to scoop Crystal Blue down at the diner, she was flying high for weeks. Mick privately thought Kendrick and Erin were taking personal delight in foiling everyone's expectations.

He pressed a hand to his chest. "I mean, Kendrick isn't even planning to tell *me*, and I was best man at his wedding. They're determined to keep the secret until the very last moment."

"Fair enough. It's been wonderful to see them so happy since finding their way back to each other."

High school sweethearts, Kendrick and Erin had broken up and left town to pursue other dreams, marrying other people. Then they'd divorced, both coming back to Eden's Ridge and ending up as teachers at the same high school where they'd fallen in love the first time. Kendrick hadn't wasted a moment winning back the love of his life.

"That it is. You know the entire high school football team has a baby pool going, right? Guessing birthdate and weight and all that jazz?"

Essie brightened. "Oh, really?"

"Sure do. If you wanna get in on that, it's the quarterback, Mason Turner, who's organizing it. Winner just gets bragging rights, because all the proceeds are going toward diapers and baby supplies, since the team knows neither of them are exactly raking it in on high school teacher salaries."

"What a wonderful idea. I'll do that."

"You have a good holiday, Mrs. Vaughn. I'll see you after the first of the year, when you're due up for your next oil change."

Essie patted his hand. "You're a good boy, Mick. Merry Christmas."

Mick waved her off and, as she was the last customer of the day, locked the door behind her with a sigh. It had been a long day, and he was looking forward to a meal with his friends before crawling into bed for eight straight. But first, home for a shower.

The three bay doors were shut against the cold, and the rest of the staff had already left for the day. Mick found his boss, Willie, settling on the creeper, preparing to slide under the 1955 Chevy Cameo Carrier he was in the process of restoring.

"I'm about to head out. You need anything?"

"Nah. Gonna spend an hour or so wrenching on this beauty before I call it for the night."

"Text me when you're done, so I know you didn't get accidentally crushed."

The old man rolled his eyes and made a grumbling noise. "Worrywart."

Maybe he was, but Willie wasn't getting any younger, and it made Mick just a little nervous how he stayed up here late most nights by himself. There wasn't a damned thing wrong with looking out for the old man. And despite Willie's grousing, Mick was pretty sure he appreciated the concern.

He headed for the side door and the employee parking lot, calling back, "You know you love me." The profane reply just made him grin. "See you tomorrow."

Mick settled into his truck, automatically checking to make sure the bakery box with the signature military-style coat of arms was undisturbed where he'd left it. He'd snuck across the street earlier in the day to Bad Boy Bakers to pick up some of the mini pear tarts that were Erin's current pregnancy craving, both as a thank you for the dinner invite and as a bribe for information. Uncle Mick wanted the inside track on news of Baby Teague.

Assured none of his coworkers had gotten into the box, he headed out. But he'd no sooner pulled onto the road than his phone vibrated with a text. Checking the readout, he saw the SOS, followed by a pin-drop with the texter's location. Revising his plans, he sent a voice text to Kendrick that he might be a little late and turned his truck south.

He found the little SUV at a relatively flat spot on the mountain road that headed out of Eden's Ridge, emergency flashers lighting up the night. Its driver was bent over, struggling with the tire iron. She straightened as he pulled up behind her, and he saw evidence of tears on her face. Little could have galvanized him faster. He leapt out.

"Ari? You okay? You hurt?"

The teenager sniffed, wiping impatiently at her wet cheeks. "I'm *fine*, except I have this stupid flat tire, and it totally doesn't matter that you taught me how to change it, because I can't get the stupid lug nuts off! What is the point of knowing how to change a tire if I'm not strong enough to get the flat one off?" she demanded.

Realizing her tears were entirely of frustration rather than something serious, he relaxed a bit. "It's a fair question. And, yeah, sometimes it's hard to combat the strength of an impact wrench. Let me help. Did you let your parents know what's going on?"

She stepped back. "No. I didn't want them to know I had a flat. I've only had the car for a *month*."

He was well aware, as Ari's mom, his foster sister Pru, had insisted he teach her all the basics of car care before allowing the teenager behind the wheel on her own.

"Flats happen. They're not gonna be mad, kiddo. Let's see what's what."

Retrieving a flashlight from his truck, he slowly rotated the rear driver's side tire, checking for the source of the damage. "You just picked up a nail. Simple puncture. I'll be able to fix that at the shop, no problem. I'll swap out to the spare for now, and you can bring it by after school tomorrow so I can get it switched back. For now, let your folks know you're running late and that I'm with you, so they don't worry."

She sniffed. "Okay."

While she texted her parents, he put his back into wrenching the nuts free and made a mental note to get her a better tire iron than the one that had come with the CRV.

Wanting to get her mind off things, he changed the subject. "So what's the latest headcount for Christmas dinner?"

"At last count, I think we've got another six fosters coming in from out of town. A lot of the solo sibs."

Ari's parents ran The Misfit Inn, which had once been home to a gigantic family of foster siblings, of which Mick had been a part. Since their foster mother, Joan Reynolds, had passed away a few years before, her four daughters had converted the old Victorian into a bed-and-breakfast and added on a spa. They'd also done a lot of work to maintain and strengthen the family ties that Joan had established over twenty-five years. It had been them to pull Mick back into the fold when he'd returned to Eden's Ridge a few years ago.

As his unofficial niece continued to reel off the list of

names, Mick made short work of swapping out to the spare. Once he had the lug nuts tightened, he lowered the jack.

"There. All set."

"Thank you! You're always so great about this sort of thing."

"You're very welcome. What sort of thing?"

"Rescuing people."

"Ah. All in a day's work." He mimed buffing his fingernails against his Carhartt jacket.

"You're coming to Christmas dinner, right?"

"I am."

"Will you be bringing a plus one this year?"

He carted the flat over to the bed of his truck and hurled it into the back. "Why would I be bringing a plus one? Anybody who I might bring also has a family and will eat with them, presumably."

"I don't know. I just thought perhaps there was a certain nurse, who's a frequent target of your particular brand of rescue, who might enjoy it. I'm just saying."

Mick rolled his eyes. "How many times do I have to tell you that Juliette and I are only friends?"

"Only because you haven't asked her out."

Because that had a little bit too much of a ring of truth to it, he put the kibosh on the conversation. "Friends," he repeated. "Go on home. I'll get this tire patched when I get to work tomorrow. Swing by the garage after school tomorrow, and I'll put it back on for you."

"Thank you." She started to throw her arms around him in her typical enthusiastic hug, then stopped. "I'm hugging you in spirit, but you smell like motor oil."

He laughed. "Fair enough. I'm on my way home for a shower."

Mick waited until she'd cranked up and pulled away before

getting back into his own truck. His brain went unerringly to the very woman Ari had mentioned. He'd meant what he'd said. From the moment she'd moved into the apartment next door, Juliette had relegated him to the Friend Zone. Never mind that he'd love to be more. His big-hearted, beautiful neighbor didn't have the bandwidth for a relationship, or so she'd said on more than one occasion when he'd asked why she wasn't dating anyone. Admittedly, she had a lot on her plate. He, of all people, understood that. So he'd contented himself with friendship for the past couple of years, doing what he could to take some of the strain off when she'd let him. Quietly doing anything else he could when she wouldn't.

But lately he'd been less and less content with that. It was coming to the point where he had to make a decision. Either he needed to take a chance on her and ask her out, and risk making their friendship weird if she said no, or he needed to turn his attention elsewhere.

The idea of the latter left him scowling.

He shook off the mood and pointed his truck toward home. He needed that shower, then he had a pot roast dinner in his future. That was something absolutely worth celebrating.

And if he happened to run into Juliette on his way in or out of the apartment... well, saying hi was just the neighborly thing to do.

JULIETTE CHEN HANDED over the precious tub of silver sulfadiazine and made a mental note that they'd need to replenish their supply. "I want to see you again in a week to assess the state of that burn. And in the meantime, try to stay away from your furnace."

Glass artist Hale Copeland didn't wither one iota beneath

her gimlet stare. "You know I've gotta go where and when the muse takes me."

The muse had taken him just shy of third-degree burns on his arm when some of the molten glass he worked with had inadvertently dripped onto his arm because of the unexpected invasion of a raccoon in his glass house.

Juliette sighed and passed over the final paperwork. "At least make the effort to plug up the hole where the raccoon got in, so you don't have a repeat. You might not be so lucky next time."

Hale saluted with his good hand and stepped out the door of the mobile medical clinic. The door slapped shut behind him, and Vicky Thornton, the nurse practitioner on duty, turned the lock. "Finally, through."

"Thank God." Juliette sank back onto a stool, letting out a long, weary sigh. She'd been going since well before dawn, and she had miles to go before she got to sleep. Or tried to, anyway.

The two women sat in companionable silence for two blessed minutes before they both started close-up procedures for the night, sterilizing supplies, stowing medications, and sanitizing every surface. It was all old hat by now, an almost meditative process that helped Juliette shift out of nursing mode. As she was organizing disinfectant supplies for tomorrow, Vicky laid a folder on the counter.

"What's this?"

"A program for financial assistance for a nurse practitioner program. You'd be an amazing one. And Lord knows, we need more medical professionals here in Wachoxee County."

Juliette left the folder on the counter, knowing that if she picked it up, Vicky would take that as encouragement. This was hardly the first time she'd floated the idea of Juliette going back to school, but the idea of trying to take on schooling for an advanced nursing degree, on top of everything else on her plate, made her want to simply lie down on the floor to nap. "I'm well aware we're in a medical desert." It was a fact that had terrified her since her family had moved here when she was thirteen. "But I just can't take on something else."

She pretended not to notice when Vicky's face fell. "Well, if you change your mind, you can count on me for a letter of recommendation."

"Thank you for that. I do appreciate your vote of confidence." And she did. Knowing that she did a good job, that she was appreciated professionally by her colleagues as well as by her patients, was often the only thing that kept her from drowning in guilt over her decision not to go into the family business.

That same guilt was why her workday wasn't over when they locked up the clinic and trudged to their cars. At least they'd been in Eden's Ridge today and the drive back to her downtown apartment wouldn't take but five minutes. She'd have time to give her geriatric potato of a dog a walk and feed him some dinner, before she turned up at Jade Palace to put in some hours there before they closed. And maybe, if she was lucky, she'd run into Mick in the hall. She could use the boost of one of his smiles and jokes to get her through the rest of the night.

But though his truck was parked outside, she saw no sign of her neighbor as she let herself into her apartment above Webster Hardware. A scrabble of claws and a yip of delight greeted her as she opened the door. Derp staggered in his usual over-enthusiastic, drunken way toward her. At some point in the past, before she'd adopted him, the rotund little dog had likely had a stroke or some other sort of brain damage, as his gait was decidedly sideways. Out of long practice, Juliette adjusted her trajectory to intercept him, scooping his thick little body up for a cuddle.

"Hey, baby boy."

Derp looked up at her with bulging, slightly crossed eyes full of adoration, his tongue permanently lolling out of one side of his mouth. Mostly brown, entirely round, with short, stubby little legs and a smushed-in face, she surmised he was at least partly pug, mixed with God knew what. He was one of those dogs who was so ugly, he was adorable, and she loved him to pieces. At nearly twelve, he was going gray around his muzzle, but he still enjoyed their short little walks.

Dropping a kiss to his head, she quickly snapped him into his harness and carried him down the stairs and out the door that led out the back of the building to the resident parking. An alley stretched down the rest of the block behind the other businesses in town. She crossed over to the grassy patch on the corner and set him down, letting him sniff to find the right spot to do his business. That done, she took him on a meandering walk around the residential block behind, letting him sniff as much as she could before urging him to the end. Time was wasting, and she needed to get to the restaurant.

Mick's truck was gone by the time she got back. Juliette squashed the disappointment and tucked Derp under one arm to trot back upstairs. She wouldn't have had time to actually talk to him, anyway. And hadn't she promised herself she'd depend on him less where she could, to make up for all those nights he was the one who fed and walked Derp when she couldn't get home in time? They were friends, nothing more. It wasn't fair to expect anything else from the man.

Settling her pup with his dinner, she refreshed the dog TV video stream he liked on YouTube and headed back out. In just the time she'd been upstairs, it seemed as if the temperature had dropped another ten degrees. She hunched into her coat and picked up her pace for the two-block walk down to Jade Palace. The neon *Open* sign glowed red in the window above the stylized pagoda palace painted on the glass. She tugged open the door and stepped inside, automatically checking to see if there were customers at the half-dozen tables out front. Only two were filled. Not bad for a Wednesday night.

The moment her attention turned to her mother, Juliette knew she was having a bad day. Sue Ellen was on her familiar stool behind the cash register at the counter. The smile she aimed at her daughter was strained around the edges and a little vacant.

"Mom? Are you okay?" Juliette skirted the counter, closing the distance as if she could somehow stop the chronic pain by her will alone.

If only.

"Oh, yes. I'm fine, honey. How was your day?"

But Juliette was too busy assessing her, noting the trembling in her limbs and the massively blown pupils that indicated an ocular migraine.

"It was fine. I'm here now. I'll take over. You should go on up to bed."

It was a sign of just how badly her mother hurt that she didn't argue. "Okay."

"Just wait here a second. I'll get Skylar to go with you."

Shoving through the swinging door to the kitchen, she spotted her baby sister, purple streaked black ponytail swinging as she loaded orders into a bag, while Tiny—aka Joe Harrington, their cook—moved with surprising speed at the stove, managing multiple orders at once.

"Hey, sis. Mom needs to go up. Why don't you help me get her upstairs, and you can hit the books some more, okay? You've got that chemistry final tomorrow, right?"

"I won't turn down the chance to get some more studying in. Let me just finish bagging up these orders."

Juliette went back out front and set a placard on the

counter indicating they'd be back in five minutes. When she went to help her mom down from the stool, Sue Ellen waved her away. Juliette curled her fingers into her palms so hard, the nails would likely leave marks. But she let her mother maintain the illusion of complete control in the public part of the restaurant. She knew that was important to her. Behind the closed kitchen door, Sue Ellen's knees started to buckle. But Juliette was there, as she always was, to catch her. Skylar raced ahead of them, opening the back door that led to the stairs up to their apartment above the restaurant. The stairs Juliette cursed on the daily as she cursed the fibromyalgia that stole her mother's vitality. It took both of them to get Sue Ellen up the flight and inside their apartment.

"To the couch," she insisted. "I'm not ready for bed yet."

Which really meant she didn't think her legs would make it that far. But Juliette didn't call her on it, just steered them toward the ancient tweed sofa.

"Do you need anything before I go back down?"

"No, I'm fine."

"I've got her," Skylar said.

Torn between wanting to stay and help, and knowing someone had to keep running the restaurant that was their family's livelihood, Juliette squeezed her sister's shoulder and did the only thing she could. Got back to work.

There were two people waiting to pick up their orders when she got back to Jade Palace. Juliette dug up a professional smile and finished the transactions. The lion's share of their income came from the takeout side of the business. It was the only reason her mom had been able to make it as long as she had, given the decline in her condition. She'd begun the business on her own thirteen years ago, after her husband had abandoned all of them, deciding that a chronic autoimmune disease and a surprise baby were too much for him to handle. It had been takeout alone to start. Only in the past five years had they added the handful of tables for dining in. Even those were bussed by the customers when they left. It was an unusual business model, but in their tiny town of three thousand, it worked.

As soon as the customers were gone, she stepped into the kitchen and confronted Tiny. "Why didn't you send her home earlier?"

Tiny, whose primary claim to fame was a stellar career as a running back for the University of Tennessee before he tore his rotator cuff more than thirty years ago, twitched those massive shoulders. "I tried. You know how your mama is. She wouldn't listen."

Yeah. She knew that.

And she knew she needed to figure out something, because her mom was having more bad days than good lately. The restaurant was surviving, but they weren't making a lot of profit. After operating costs, they had just a little bit more than they needed for living expenses. Juliette herself wasn't taking payment for the hours she put in, and Skylar wasn't getting as much as she deserved because the rest was going to overhead and rent and all the things. Juliette needed to dig into the books to see if she could massage the budget to find money for a new stove. They were on borrowed time with this one, and it was an essential expense. They couldn't have a restaurant without it.

Tiny put a plate in front of her. "Beef lo mien. I know you. You haven't eaten yet."

Juliette sighed. "I haven't. Thank you, Tiny."

She got through the last couple of hours of the night, taking and filling orders until closing time at eight-thirty. Tiny was the one who chased her out when she tried to stick around to clean up. It was a sign of exactly how exhausted she was that she didn't argue with him.

Like mother, like daughter.

At least she had only two more days until she was actually off her primary job for longer than a weekend. The mobile clinic would be closed for several days, owing to the Christmas holiday. Not that she'd get a chance to actually rest. That luxury was for other people who didn't have so many responsibilities. But at least she'd be able to sleep in before taking her turn at Jade Palace.

The dream of that sleep filled her mind on the walk home, propelling her upstairs to her apartment.

"Just a little while longer…"

She unlocked the door and pushed it open, then stopped dead as she took in the chaos awaiting inside.

"Oh, no."

TWO

"You're not gonna give me even a *little* hint?"

On the other side of the rectangular table, Kendrick extended his arm along the back of his wife's chair and looked smug. "Nope. We're not telling." They were a good-looking couple, with Kendrick's broad shoulders, medium brown skin, and bright smile a complement to his wife's blonde, blue-eyed, former cheerleader, girl-next-door beauty.

Mick made a big show of his dramatic exhalation. "Fine."

As he'd wanted, Erin giggled.

Sobering, he straightened. "But seriously, everything's good? Healthy?"

Laying a hand over her baby bump, she beamed. "Everything's exactly on track and as it should be."

"Good. We're all looking forward to meeting Baby Teague in April. You know the kid's gonna have his or her own Wildcats jersey no matter what, right?"

"I mean, the fact that the team gifted me one that says Mrs. Coach Teague on the back was a bit of a clue," Erin pointed out.

"Gotta keep it in the family." Kendrick pushed back from the table. When his wife started to rise, too, he waved her back down. "No ma'am. You sit. You're doing important work incubating a human right now. Mick and I have the dishes."

"I'm certainly not gonna argue."

They made quick work of the mess, putting the leftovers away, loading the dishwasher, and scrubbing up the remaining pots and pans. Because he had an early morning, and because he could see Erin already starting to nod off a little at the table, Mick made his excuses.

"I should be getting on. Thank y'all so much for dinner. I'm never gonna turn down a home-cooked meal. Especially when I didn't have to make it." He hugged his friends and reached for his coat.

"Oh! Before you go." Erin grabbed an envelope from her purse. "You know that band, Lost Ridge Ramblers?"

"Yeah. They're one of my favorites."

"Well, we booked tickets for a show they're putting on at an inn up in Merry Falls, North Carolina this weekend. After how I'm feeling right now, I absolutely cannot be in a car again. Just going to Johnson City for my doctor's appointment nearly did me in."

Kendrick sobered. "We had to pull over twice for her to vomit on the way home."

"Anyway, there's no way I can tolerate nearly three hours there and back on those super twisty roads, and we don't want the tickets to go to waste, so we want to give them to you," Erin finished.

Mick was both flattered and horrified. "That's incredibly generous of you, but let me buy the tickets from you. I know they must've cost a fortune."

Kendrick waved that off. "Consider it an early Christmas present. We also got a room at the inn that's hosting the show.

It's in some kind of partnership with The Misfit Inn, so that was some kind of trade thing Kennedy arranged. Nothing to pay anybody back for."

Staring at his foster brother, Mick tried to find the catch. "Are you sure?" He knew they wouldn't be able to do a whole lot of extra stuff because of the baby coming, both because of money and time.

Erin cuddled into her husband. "We're sure."

Kendrick plucked the envelope from his wife's hand and shoved it into Mick's. "Enjoy it, brother."

Stunned at their generosity, he could only nod. "Thank you. I certainly will."

As he shrugged into his coat, Erin added in a too-casual tone, "You've got two tickets, so maybe you can take a friend who also likes the band."

Not fooled by her this-is-no-big-deal face, Mick shot her some side-eye, knowing she was talking about Juliette, who also loved the band. "We'll see."

But they'd planted the idea in his head such that it circled around up there the whole drive back to his place. Juliette would have several days off, starting this weekend. He knew her work schedule because he so frequently helped with Derp. What were the odds she'd be able to get away to go? He couldn't remember the last time she'd done something for herself, purely for the fun of it. The trip would certainly do her good. Maybe he'd just stop by her place to see if she was still awake and mention it. Because if she could go, there'd be arrangements to be made.

Faint sounds of music greeted him at the top of the stairs. So she was definitely still awake. His hand hesitated just shy of the door as he registered *what* music was playing. Gloria Gaynor's "I Will Survive."

Oh, no. Oh damn.

Juliette only pulled that out when it had been a particularly shittastic day.

He knocked, calling out her name for good measure. When the door swung open a few moments later, the first thing he noticed were the bloodshot, puffy eyes that said she'd been crying.

"What happened? What's wrong? Whose ass needs kicking?"

Instinctively, he reached for her, wanting to pull her in for a hug or some other kind of comfort, but she shied away.

"No, don't touch me. There's poop."

"What?"

"The Roomba." She waved a hand in the vague direction of the kitchen nook, where he spotted the partially disassembled robot vacuum lying on its back like some kind of turtle on a towel on the kitchen table. "The damn thing is supposed to recognize poop and stop. But the detectors didn't detect, and I've just finished cleaning the floors."

He realized the sofa was askew, and the washable rug was wadded up in the corner.

"It was bad," she rasped. "Like one of those internet memes bad. And I'm never going to be able to get it clean. I'll be stuck with a poopy vacuum forever."

Her lower lip wobbled, as if she were about to start crying again. She was so clearly at the end of her rope, and everything in him wanted to cuddle this woman because he was crazy about her, and he just wanted to make her feel better. But that wasn't the sort of relationship they had, so he focused on what he could take off her plate.

"Oh, God. Okay. Stop. I'll fix the Roomba."

"It's not your responsibility."

"Juliette, I have more mechanical capabilities than you do. Mechanic, right? I've been taking things apart and putting them back together since I was five. I'll fix the Roomba. You have done enough for the night."

"But..."

"You're gonna sit down, and you're gonna have a glass of wine with an emergency episode of *Ted Lasso*. Then you're gonna go to bed, because you're about to drop."

For a long moment, she just stared at him. Then she whispered, "Okay."

Oh, baby.

He gave in to the urge to squeeze her shoulder, then went to wrestle the sofa back into place while she washed her hands. Realizing there was no slightly drunk sausage with legs underfoot, he glanced up. "Where's Derp?"

"Locked in the bathroom."

Mick was almost afraid to ask. "Does he need a bath?"

"No, he managed to stay out of everything."

"Okay." Because she wasn't showing any sign of moving on her own, he gently steered her toward the sofa and nudged her onto it, draping the fleece throw from the back over her lap. Grabbing the remote, he turned on the TV and navigated to *Ted Lasso*. It was a comfort watch she'd seen dozens of times, so it didn't really matter which episode he queued up. He hit Resume and went to liberate the dog.

Derp gave a joyful burble at the sight of him. As always, Mick huffed a laugh and scooped him up. "Hey, pal. You need to go cuddle your mama. She's having a bad night."

Derp nodded in agreement, his tongue lolling. Pup safely deposited into Juliette's lap, Mick poured a glass of wine from the single bottle she rationed out each week and carried it back to her, squatting down in front of her and wrapping her cold, slim fingers around the basin.

"I've got this. You just relax."

On the screen, the entire football team hung over one teammate's shoulder, waiting to see if the woman he'd been messaging through an online dating app would agree to meet in person. Mick put himself to work, scooping up the rug and getting it into the wash. She probably wouldn't remember to swap it over to the dryer tonight, but he could pop over tomorrow and do it at some point. Then he adiosed all components of the Roomba to his own place. Juliette wasn't wrong. Getting all the poop out of the rollers and wheels and inner mechanisms was going to be a challenge. He didn't want her worrying over it while he figured out what to do. If worse came to worst, he'd buy her a new one and find a way to switch them out on the down low.

Washing his own hands, he went back to her apartment where, on screen, characters Sam and Rebecca had just realized they were each other's mystery date. He sank down next to her on the sofa, pleased to see the mostly empty wine glass clutched in her hand as she absently stroked a snoring Derp's soft belly. Her dark brown eyes were heavy, and her shoulders were no longer hitched with tension. Maybe she would actually sleep tonight.

He wished he could pull her against him. If ever someone needed a good snuggle, she did. She was hanging on by a thread, in desperate need of a break. But he knew if he said a word about the prospect of this trip, she'd turn him down. She'd make excuses and say she couldn't go. If there was a chance in hell of actually getting her out of town, he'd have to go ahead and make arrangements for everything before he even asked her. So, as Rebecca stood on her doorstep with Sam at the end of their non-date and insisted the two of them were a terrible idea, Mick settled in to scheme.

ON FRIDAY, Juliette finished what she thought of as the changing of the guard in record time, going over open cases with Malika Hobbes, the travel nurse who'd be filling in on the skeleton crew for emergencies until Juliette was due back on rotation later next week, after Christmas. By three o'clock, she was blessedly free and had at least a couple of hours before she needed to check in at Jade Palace for the Friday night rush. She was torn between the idea of taking an actual nap so that she was awake to appreciate the time off and doing something else. Like... reading a book for longer than a chapter at a time. Or maybe even stopping by At Your Leisure, the bookstore with a wine bar inside that was one of her favorite places in Eden's Ridge.

Derp would get his walk first, then she'd see how she felt. Maybe a short jaunt around the block would invigorate her.

Her little pup scrambled up from his kitchen bed and ambled over to her as soon as she opened the door. She scooped him up for their ritual love fest and only then realized that her rug had been put back down. In fact, the entire living room had been put back together. The Roomba sat on the table, a folded piece of paper on top of it. Tucking Derp beneath one arm, she opened the note.

"All scrubbed out and good as new. Got rid of the accumulation of hair slowing down the wheels, too. — M."

Mick, of course.

"What a sweetheart he is," she murmured to the dog.

"I try."

Startled, she whirled to find him leaning against the doorjamb, grinning. That bright, easy smile didn't do a thing to slow the heart thudding in her chest. Juliette clutched the dog closer. "Thank you for all this."

"It was no problem. And I'm about to do you one better. Go pack a bag."

"Excuse me?"

"We're going on a road trip."

Had she stepped into some kind of parallel universe? "What are you talking about?"

"Because my very pregnant sister-in-law cannot be in a car for longer than five minutes without hurling, I was gifted a pair of tickets for a show tonight with the Lost Ridge Ramblers down in Merry Falls, North Carolina, and you're the perfect person to come with me. You need a break in a big way, and I don't want to take anybody who doesn't appreciate their music as much as I do."

The swell of excitement was instant. A trip to see her favorite band with arguably one of her favorite people? Not that Mick was aware of his status in that echelon. But the sinking disappointment hit her moments later. "You're so sweet to offer, Mick, but I can't possibly go. I have nobody to look after Derp. I can't just dump him on my mom and sister. And the weekend is our busiest time at the restaurant."

"Derp will be staying with my brother, Declan, and his family. You know how much he and Hagrid adore each other."

"That dog's *head* is bigger than Derp!" Not that she'd ever seen the Newfoundland mix be aggressive.

"They're besties. Or want to be. Everything's all set. He's gonna be living his best life and chilling with a fenced-in yard to run around in and a fireplace to nap in front of."

Bless Mick's stubborn, well-intentioned heart. "That's lovely of you to arrange, but I still can't leave my family to fend for themselves at the restaurant."

Mick just held up a hand. "Got you covered. We'll be back tomorrow. My siblings are all taking a turn, popping in two-by-two to cover three-hour shifts, run the register, bag up orders and whatever so that we don't have to rush back. I already worked it out with your mom."

There was so much to react to in everything he'd just said, but the part her brain latched onto was, "You talked to my mom?"

"Sure did. She told me I was a good boy, and under no circumstances was I to let you say no."

Juliette closed her eyes for a moment, fighting the urge to wince. Her mom probably thought this was some kind of romantic date trip or something. She was on Juliette's case about dating all the time. As if there was time for that.

Then her brain caught up to the rest, and her eyes popped open. "Overnight?"

"Yeah, the show won't be over until late, so no reason to drive back on twisty mountain roads in the middle of the night. We've already got a room at the inn."

She opened her mouth, her mind already offering more excuses why she had to refuse this incredible offer, but he interrupted her.

"It's just a day, Juliette. Twenty-four hours for you to breathe. Your rug is already clean, everything's put back together from Poopageddon. There's no reason you can't go."

Juliette stared at him. This sweet, wonderful man had anticipated every single objection she'd make and orchestrated solutions to cover all of them, just so that she could go do this crazy, impulsive thing. Because he knew her well enough to know that she didn't *do* crazy and impulsive.

When she still didn't speak, his cocky self-assurance faded. "I mean, if you don't *want* to go, that's a whole separate thing. I know I'm being hella presumptive here. I just know how much you like the Lost Ridge Ramblers, and I thought... Well, I guess I should've asked first."

"We both know if you had, I'd have said no." She didn't know why she admitted that, except that he'd taken her so by surprise, she felt compelled to be honest.

"There is that," he admitted. But there was no judgment or resignation in his tone. He knew her, and he seemed entirely okay with who she was, messes and all. It was a big part of why she valued him as a friend.

"Why would you do all of this for me?" She couldn't help her natural suspicion. In her experience, men simply weren't that thoughtful, and they definitely didn't do things for her or her family.

"Because you need it." The simple weight of those words settled between them, vibrating with the ring of utter truth.

Juliette wanted to read into it. Wanted this to mean that he cared for her beyond friendship. But from bitter experience, she knew better. And that was why she'd never let on that she felt more for this man than simple friendship. Why she'd never let him see what all his little kindnesses meant to her. Because she didn't want to ask for more, only to lose him entirely.

He was her fun. The micro-dose of it she allowed herself amid the chaos of her normal world. The prospect of getting out of town, away from that chaos for a day, sounded heavenly. And she really did love the band. Was she really going to turn down this amazing gift?

No, she wasn't.

"You are such an incredible friend, and I am lucky to have you."

The cocky smile was back, making his green eyes sparkle. "Of course you are. Now, go pack. We've gotta hoof it if we're gonna make it there by showtime."

Laughing, she turned to do as she'd been told.

THREE

"I can't believe it's snowing." Juliette's tone was full of awe.

"Me either." Mick peered through the fall of fat, swirling flakes with a bit more trepidation. The weather was the one thing he hadn't checked in the course of all his planning and preparation. It wasn't like they never saw snow in Northeast Tennessee, but this felt more like late January than mid-December. He was grateful that his truck had four-wheel drive and aggressive tires, and that they were only a half hour out from their destination according to the GPS.

Beside him, Juliette's phone sounded with an incoming text. At her rolling laugh, he glanced over. "What?"

"Declan just sent a picture of Derp and Hagrid snuggled up together, passed out in front of the fireplace. Apparently, they've already worn each other out running around the yard."

Mick's lips curved. "I told you he'd be living his best life."

"Yeah, you did. And my sister has already texted to say that Ari showed up and is doing great with the dinner rush." She sighed. "You thought of everything. Thank you again."

He looked over just long enough to take in those gorgeous, almond-shaped eyes. "You're welcome again."

They'd been gone less than three hours, and he could already see the weights sliding off her. She was a curious mix of tired from the long week and wired with excitement over the concert, but the strain that was her constant companion was definitely significantly less. That made him bold enough to push a little. "Can I ask you something?"

"Sure."

"Why is it that you take all of this on yourself? You're essentially working two jobs, running two households."

He caught her shrug in his periphery. "Because there's nobody else to do it. You already know my mom is chronically ill. That was a big part of why I went into nursing. To have a better idea of how I can best help her."

"I know your dad isn't in the picture. At least, you've never mentioned him."

"He bailed a couple of years after my sister was born. The surprise late pregnancy significantly exacerbated Mom's condition, and it turned out that a late baby and a chronic autoimmune disease that meant Mom couldn't do all the things she used to do were too much for him to handle. So we moved to Eden's Ridge to start over when I was thirteen. It's been the three of us ever since." She stated it all in a flat, emotionless tone, like a report of the weather or the recitation of a recipe. But Mick knew there had to be more to it than that.

He recognized that she was the glue holding everything together for her family. Skylar was a grade behind Ari, so she'd be about sixteen. Juliette would've been ten when she was born. Reading between the lines, he realized she'd likely been juggling all these plates, taking on everything her mother hadn't been able to, for all those years since. Probably before they'd moved to Eden's Ridge. And she'd had nobody to take care of *her* since then.

It broke his heart and made him want to try all the more to make sure that she had an incredible time this weekend. If she wasn't going to get frequent time off—and with her life circumstances, that was simply a reality right now—he wanted to make the most of the trip they had.

"Well, for the next twenty-four hours, anyway, none of those responsibilities are yours. So your mission, should you choose to accept it, is to be selfish for once in your life and throw yourself into this weekend with hedonistic abandon."

She snorted a laugh. "I'm not sure I'd have the first idea how to do that."

"It begins with trusting that everybody back home has your back and putting that phone away once we get there. I'm not sure there's great cell coverage in that little pocket of mountains, anyway. I remember reading on the website that even though it's only a few miles from town, the inn itself is accessible only by one winding mountain road. And you know how reception can be in some of the deep valleys and hollers."

"True enough. I make a solemn vow to not be obsessively glued to my phone."

Mick nodded to himself in satisfaction. "That's a good start."

"As you are my official fun guide this weekend, I expect further coaching points as we go."

That had him grinning again. "I can definitely do that."

Juliette leaned forward, peering through the windshield. "Man, I have never seen it come down like this in December."

"Good thing this is the south. Whatever comes down now should be gone by tomorrow afternoon, in plenty of time to come home." He hoped. He had no idea how cold it had been down here in the previous days. Cold, judging by the wall of white rising on both sides of the road where the snow was already accumulating against the ground.

Big, Griswald-style Christmas lights emerged from the white like a beacon, draping the sign for The Merry Falls Inn. With relief, Mick took the final turn into the drive to the inn. The building itself was nestled among the trees, two stories of rustic splendor, with porches stretching along both levels, all the way across the front. The railings were draped with garland and more lights. Each window was accented by a beribboned wreath. There was even a live Christmas tree decorated out front, soaring more than twenty feet.

"Wow, they really take Christmas seriously around here," Juliette observed.

"I think that's kind of their thing. I read something on the website about them celebrating year round."

Following the small signs, he parked his truck in the lot behind the inn. The two of them grabbed their overnight bags and made their way carefully through the snow to the door. They stomped the worst of it off their shoes, then stepped inside. It wasn't quite kitschy enough to feel like Santa's work-shop, but it wasn't far off. The holiday theme continued, with evergreen boughs and ribbon and lights *everywhere*.

An older woman hurried around from the counter. "Welcome to the Merry Falls Inn! I'm Lucy Gibbins, the owner."

Mick flashed a smile. "Hi. Mick Routledge. We're looking to check in."

"You're here for the concert?"

"We are."

"It's just about to start. Leave your bags here, and head on into the pub. I'll see that your stuff makes it up to your room."

"Thank you, Ms. Gibbins. We really appreciate it." Juliette put her bag down.

"Of course, dearie! Enjoy the show."

Mick added his bag to the pile, and they made their way down the hall Lucy had indicated. A pair of French doors were open to a large space that took up one end of the lower floor of the inn. At a glance, maybe sixty people were scattered among the tables around the stage set up on the far side of the room. The whole place was done up in warm, dark wood. A stone fireplace held a crackling blaze on one wall, and the long-polished bar looked like something that had come straight from Ireland.

They ducked into an empty booth. Moments later, a server appeared.

"Are you here just for drinks or would you like food?"

Mick's stomach growled, the road snacks they'd packed having long since worn off. "Food, definitely."

"Great. Here are a couple of menus. What can I get you to drink in the meantime?"

They gave their orders, and the girl scurried away. Juliette glanced toward the stage, then back at him. "You should come over here so we can both see the stage. You won't see a thing from that side."

When she scooted over to make room for him on the opposite side of the booth, Mick couldn't come up with a single reason to refuse, even if being pressed that close to her would be its own form of torture. "Fair point."

He slid out of his seat and joined her on the other side. It wasn't a big booth, and he wasn't a small guy. "You okay? Got room enough?"

"Half-Asian, remember? I'm tiny. Occasionally, that's handy."

She was, but he could still feel the heat of her leg pressed up against his, and he noticed every minute shift of her body as she continued to study the menu. He was so distracted by her closeness, he didn't even manage to read the menu by the time the server returned with their drinks. So he just ordered a burger, figuring that was standard pub fare and probably listed. The server took their orders and retrieved the menus just as the crowd began to cheer.

The Lone Ridge Ramblers filed onto the stage and picked up their instruments. The show was about to begin.

"WE'RE ABOUT to wrap for the night, but we've got one more for you."

A palpable sense of anticipation settled over the crowd as Brooke Baxter, the lead vocalist, nodded to her bandmates. The twang of a banjo rippled through the air, its familiar rhythm as fast-paced and invigorating as a rushing mountain stream. This was one of Juliette's favorites. The fiddle soon joined, seamlessly weaving its high-pitched melodies with the banjo's plucky undertones. The pulse of the stand-up bass resonated in Juliette's chest, drawing her in, even before Brooke began to sing, her voice raw and emotive as she told the tale of love lost and times gone by in the Appalachian hills. As with much of bluegrass, the song was somehow bright and poignant, with a touch of melancholy, full of vivid imagery and harmonies that painted a picture and tugged at her heart.

Beside her, Mick tapped his feet to the rhythm, his leg and shoulder brushing steadily against hers as he bobbed his head to the music. Juliette let herself sway with him, dancing a little in the booth. A handful of other patrons were out of their seats, full on dancing as the song built to its climax, the instruments conversing in a frenzied yet harmonious dialogue. And then it ended, the final note lingering in the momentary hush before the crowd went wild with applause.

Her whole body was revved, but she could feel the fatigue lingering just underneath. The moment she stopped moving, stopped focusing, she was going to crash.

Up on stage, the band took another bow as Lucy took the mic.

"Let's have another round of applause for the fabulous Lost Ridge Ramblers!"

The audience was happy to comply, and there were calls for "Encore!" and "More!"

Lucy lifted her hands for silence. "I'm afraid that's all we have time for tonight. But before any of you leaves, I have an announcement to make. This is most especially pertinent to those of you who did not book accommodations for the night. The snow has continued at an unprecedented level, and I am sorry to tell you that the pass is blocked. We've had two feet come down. There's no way to clear the road and, unfortunately, only one way in or out. Nobody's getting out here tonight."

A murmur of concern swept the crowd.

"Those of you who have rooms certainly are fine. Those of you who do not, please come speak to me. I promise, we're going to make sure everyone has somewhere to sleep tonight. Really sorry about all of this, folks. None of us expected this kind of weather in North Carolina in December."

"Thank God we have a room," Mick muttered.

"Seriously." Juliette clutched the key Lucy had brought to them during the show. "Let's get out of here."

Mick slid out of the booth, and she found she instantly missed the warmth of him beside her. Which was ridiculous. They fell into the flow of people moving out of the pub and toward the stairs up to the second-floor rooms, discussing the performance and which songs had been their favorite.

"It's always 'Whippoorwill's Lament' for me. It just hits me right in the feels," he insisted.

"'Bridges of Blue Ridge' for me. Those harmonies are killer." As they reached the door to room 11, Juliette slid the key into the lock and opened it.

She stepped inside, automatically hitting the light switch beside the door. Then she stopped dead.

Mick ran into the back of her, grabbing her by the arms when she started to flail forward. "Sorry. Is something wrong?"

"Um." Nothing was wrong, exactly.

He skirted around her, taking in the very tiny room and clearly coming to the same realization. "Oh."

This inn was not like a commercial hotel with two queen or double beds. There was one bed. A double. Which meant they'd be sharing.

"Well, I can—"

Before he made some absurd offer to sleep on the floor or something—not really practical considering how small the room was to begin with, Juliette interrupted. "It's fine. We'll fit."

Her bag was set neatly on the little luggage rack, and his lay at the foot of the bed.

"Right." He scooped a hand through his thick, dark brown hair. "Do you want first dibs on the bathroom?"

"If you don't mind."

"Go ahead."

Grabbing her bag, she disappeared into the bath. It also wasn't huge, but it was comfortable, with a clawfoot tub and warm bronze fixtures. She carefully laid out her toiletries and changed into her pajamas, grateful she'd packed for cold weather. After she'd brushed her teeth and arranged her things with military precision, she figured she'd wasted enough time and had to go back out and face this situation.

When she stepped out of the bathroom, he'd already

changed into some flannel pajama pants and a t-shirt that clung to his chest in a way that hid absolutely none of the muscles she tried not to think about.

"All done?"

His voice snapped her out of her immobility. Mortified, she realized she'd been staring at that chest. "Oh, yes. Sorry. I think I'm a little overtired."

"Crawl on into bed. I won't be long."

He'd shut himself in the bathroom before she'd managed to convince her brain that he wasn't coming to bed *with* her the way that sounded.

Get a grip, woman. You are a grown adult. You can share a bed with a friend for nothing but sleeping.

She tucked her bag back on the luggage rack and climbed into the bed, luxuriating for a minute on the soft, soft sheets and comfy pillow. The bathroom door opened a minute later, and Mick stepped out, putting his bag in the corner and turning out the light before crossing the room. The mattress immediately sank under his weight, rolling her toward his bigger bulk.

"Shit. Sorry. I know I'm taking up more than my fair share here."

"It's fine. Maybe if we both lay on our sides."

"Cool."

They shifted around and ended up facing each other. They weren't touching, but Juliette was aware of every inch of him mere centimeters away.

"I'm really sorry about this." His low voice was soft in the dark.

"It's fine."

"You keep saying that, but is it really?"

She had a sense there was more to the question than their immediate situation. "I've learned to make it so. But this is a little weird for me. I haven't shared a bed in any capacity with anybody since my fiancé dumped me."

Her mouth snapped shut. That was so not the confession she'd meant to make.

Mick was silent for a long moment. "I didn't know you'd been engaged."

The intimacy of the dark and the shared bed encouraged all kinds of whispered confessions, and Juliette found she wanted to tell him. "We dated back in college. He proposed senior year. We were planning the wedding for the year after. But ultimately, he decided that my family was too much for him, and he didn't really want to take all of us on. He loved me. Not everything attached to me."

Mick swore. "That's not love."

"I figured that out in a hurry." Though she still felt a little throb at the old hurt. "I'm just glad he broke things off before we actually got married. A divorce would have been worse. But yeah, that's part of why I don't date. It used to be a bigger part. Now, it's really that I just don't feel like I have the time and energy to put into a relationship. I really can't put anything else on my plate."

"Relationships aren't supposed to be obligations. They're supposed to be support. Helping take things *off* your plate. Maybe you've just been dating the wrong guys." The low murmur of his voice was soothing, even if his words were not.

She thought of everything Mick had done for her. His kindness. His observant nature. His unwavering good cheer. He was there for her in ways no guy ever had been. So yeah, maybe she had been dating the wrong guys. But she didn't want to screw up their friendship and lose him by trying to date him and having it fail. If that was even where he was going with this. Which he probably wasn't. She was just imagining things in the dark, in the strange intimacy of a shared bed.

"Maybe."

Because she didn't want to continue this line of conversation, she rolled over, positioning herself at the edge of the mattress where she wasn't touching him. "Goodnight, Mick."

After a long moment, he rolled over himself. "Goodnight, Juliette."

FOUR

Mick woke slowly to warmth and softness, a delicious, comforting sensation that encouraged him to linger in the liminal space between sleep and consciousness. That warmth moved south, and his morning wood made a bid for attention. Yeah, he could get on board with that. On a sigh, he shifted and found himself tangled up.

Confused, he opened his eyes and registered two things at once. One, he wasn't at home. Two, he wasn't alone in this bed.

His bedmate snuggled closer, nuzzling a cold nose against his throat, and Mick got a whiff of a familiar floral shampoo.

Juliette.

She was wrapped around him like a vine, her legs twined with his, her arm draped low across his stomach, perilously close to his erection. Her soft breath stroked along his throat with each exhalation, which wasn't doing anything to relieve the issue under the covers. And the total relaxation of her body against his told him she was still fully asleep.

He didn't want to wake her, he just needed the chance to get himself under control. Easier said than done. Slowly, he reached for her hand, gently curling his fingers around hers and inching her palm into less dangerous territory. When she didn't rouse, he relaxed again, enjoying himself for as long as it lasted.

The room was frigid. A quick glance at the bedside clock showed a blank display. Power outage, apparently.

He wondered how long ago that had happened, and whether the cold had driven her to snuggle him or if it had been something else.

She can't be held responsible for anything she did in her sleep. It doesn't mean anything.

But damn, he wanted it to. He loved having her close like this. Loved seeing her fully relaxed. Somehow, he doubted she slept this deeply in her own bed at home. In fact, she was probably normally up by now, getting started on the eleven thousand things on her to-do list, even though it was Saturday. The woman didn't know the meaning of the word rest.

But here, there was nothing they had to do. No alarm. Nowhere to be. At least not until the roads were clear. So he'd leave her be until she woke up on her own.

Curled around her, Mick watched the gray light of dawn brighten and creep across the room. And if he turned his head so that his cheek brushed against the silk of her hair, well, there was no one to call him on it.

With a sleepy purr, she snuggled closer for a few moments before tensing her whole body in a long, languid stretch. She lifted her head, and he met those liquid brown eyes, still mostly closed. At the sight of him, her lips curved into a sleepy smile that lit him up like the sunrise.

"Mornin'," he rasped.

The sound of his voice shattered the moment of connection.

Eyes going wide, Juliette jerked back from him, fumbling as she tried to untangle her legs. "Oh, God. I'm sorry."

So much for their morning cuddle. Mick scrubbed a hand over his stubbled face and yawned. "'S fine."

She sat bolt upright, the covers falling to her waist to reveal the sweatshirt and flannel pants she'd slept in. Nothing at all about the outfit was salacious, but the sleep-rumpled look of her had his morning wood stirring again with ideas of stripping her out of her pajamas and rumpling her a whole lot more.

Down, boy.

Mick began mentally reciting engine parts, trying to will it away. The last thing he wanted was to make her feel more awkward.

Juliette wrapped both arms around herself. "It's freezing in here."

He sat up himself, careful to keep the blankets over his lap. "I think the power's out."

They both reached for their phones on the bedside tables.

"Dead," she reported.

"Mine, too." He tested the lamp. Nothing. "Definitely no power."

"I wonder if the road is open."

"Only one way to find out. Let's head downstairs."

They both slid out of bed, dancing awkwardly around each other to retrieve their clothes. She shut herself into the bathroom to change, clearly embarrassed. He quickly donned his own clothes, wondering if he should say something to try to put her more at ease. But in the end, he said nothing when she stepped out, fully dressed.

Downstairs, they found quite a few of the other guests milling around, congregating around the fireplace in the main lobby, where a blaze cheerfully snapped in the hearth.

Lucy smiled as they strode up to her. "Good mornin'. I apologize for the cold. Fresh fires have been laid in all the fireplaces, and we're working on getting our generators going. As soon as that's sorted, we'll get started on some breakfast."

"Is there anything I can do to help?" Juliette asked.

It was so like her to take on more work on what was supposed to be a vacation.

Lucy patted her shoulder. "No, honey. We've got it under control."

"What's the news regarding the road closure?" Mick asked.

"Not good, I'm afraid. We had another six inches of snow last night, which is outrageous for this part of the country and this time of year. Add to that, multiple power lines are down, one directly on the road, so that's going to slow down anything getting plowed until it can be safely removed. The whole county's scrambling. We aren't prepared for this level of snow. They're gonna get to us, but it definitely won't be today, and might not be tomorrow, either. Compared to the rest of town, we're pretty remote."

Juliette's brows drew together. "So we're stuck here until Monday?"

"There's a strong possibility," Lucy warned. "But we've got plenty of food, firewood, and supplies. We won't starve, and we won't freeze. If y'all want some coffee, there's some going on a percolator on a campfire stove in the main part of the lodge. That'll get us started until the generators are online."

Even as she spoke, the overhead lights flickered on.

Everyone cheered.

Lucy clapped her hands. "Now we're cooking. Or can, anyway. I'm gonna go get started on some breakfast. Y'all enjoy yourselves."

As the older woman strode away, Juliette bit her lip. "We weren't prepared to be gone that long."

Mick risked a stroke down her back, wanting to comfort. "It'll be fine. Everybody who's helping will keep pitching in. It won't be a big deal for Derp to stay another day or two with Declan's family, and I've got plenty of family who can keep rotating in at the restaurant until we can get home. They'll understand."

When she continued to look uncertain, he began steering her toward the stairs. "Now that the power's back up, we can charge our phones. Let's go plug them up and get coffee while we wait. Then we can call home and let everybody know what's going on."

She lifted those big brown eyes to his and exhaled. "Okay."

He'd make sure she did what she needed to set her own mind at ease, then he planned to spend the rest of the day helping her make the most of the unexpected time off.

AS SOON AS she'd downed her first cup of coffee, Juliette retrieved her phone. There was no signal inside the inn, so she bundled up against the lingering cold and retreated out onto the long, open gallery off their room. Snow had drifted against the wall and the railing, leaving a narrow path down the center. No one else was out here.

She paced the length of the gallery until she found a spot where she had a couple of bars. Then she called her sister, in case her mother was still sleeping. Although, by this time of day, they ought to be prepping to open for lunch.

Skylar answered after the first ring. "Well, well. Look who it is. How is the trip going?"

Understanding she needed to give a little before she got into the meat of things, Juliette admitted, "The show last night was amazing."

Skylar scoffed. "I don't care about the band. I want to know how things are going with the hunky mechanic."

Juliette's brain immediately flashed back to this morning, how she'd woken up wrapped around Mick like kudzu. Her blood heated at the memory of his nearness, at that sleepy, rumbled greeting. She'd been completely plastered against all those muscles she tried not to think about him having. And he definitely hadn't been complaining. Then again, she had no idea when he'd woken up.

Despite all that, she was compelled to correct her sister's assumption. "Things aren't like that between Mick and me. I've told you that before."

"So you keep saying. But methinks the lady doth protest too much. The man likes you, Juliette. He took you away for the weekend. Read the room, girl. When are you going to do something about it?"

Last night would've been that opportunity, if she'd been so inclined. They'd shared a bed. A million and one fantasies about that had scrolled through her brain while she was trying to fall asleep. She'd lain awake long into the night, listening to the sound of his breathing, and being lulled by it, even as she'd thought about what it would be like to roll over and touch him. What it would be like to have those big, work-roughened hands on her.

Apparently, her sleeping self had a lot less restraint than the waking version.

Right. Time to change the subject.

"None of this is why I called. I don't know if you looked at the weather report, but we've gotten a crazy lot of snow up here. More than two full feet."

"Two feet! That's nuts. I'm so jealous. That's grounds for a snow day, for sure."

"Yeah, well, we're stuck here because the roads are closed, and power lines are down. The whole county is under a massive blanket of snow. I may not get home until Monday."

"That's totally fine. Everything is going great here. It's solid proof that you can, in fact, take some time away, once in a while. I personally think that this snowstorm is a fortuitous occurrence. You are trapped at a romantic mountain inn, sharing a room with the hot muscley mechanic. If you don't do something about that while you're there, I'm going to be incredibly disappointed."

"You are utterly shameless." And thank God she didn't know they'd actually shared a *bed*. "Are you sure everything is okay there? How's Mom?"

"Better today. Had a good night's sleep, so she's hurting less. We have it under control, Miss Control Freak. I'm out for Christmas break, so I've got more flexibility. Now go do something radical and have fun. Preferably of the naked variety."

"Skylar!"

"What? Getting laid would no doubt do you some good."

Cheeks burning hot enough to steam in the cold morning, Juliette sniffed. "I'm going to pretend you didn't say that."

"Whatever helps you sleep at night, sister dear. Now go have fun and don't worry about us. We're good. Enjoy the break."

"I'm sure I will. If anything goes wrong..."

Skylar interrupted. "If anything goes wrong, you're too far away to do anything about it. So we won't be calling you. You are officially ordered to enjoy yourself."

"But I..."

Dead air was her only answer. Skylar had hung up on her.

Juliette stared at the phone in affront. "Have fun. Easy for you to say. You don't have the weight of the world on your shoulders."

But her sister wasn't wrong. If anything did go wrong, what *could* she do from here? Not much. Which meant there really wasn't anything to do *but* have fun. She was pretty sure she needed a remedial course on how to do that. Good thing she was here with a man who knew how to embrace that aspect of life.

As she made her way back inside and downstairs, she thought of the other thing her sister had said. Was Mick truly interested in her? She thought she'd seen signs of interest from time to time, flickers of potential chemistry. Certainly, she felt it herself, even if she didn't let herself acknowledge it. Being close to him for this sustained period of time, all those messy feelings of attraction and arousal had woken inside her. Combined with her very real affection for him, it was a lot harder to remember all the reasons she hadn't pursued anything. The biggest one was, and always had been, that she didn't have the bandwidth to think about a relationship.

She thought of what he'd said last night, about how relationships were meant to be support, not obligation. Her perception had been strongly colored by her past history with both her ex and her father. She understood that.

Mick wouldn't be like either of them. He was a man who believed in offering help and support. This weekend was a case in point. A lot of that was because of his own background. She didn't know much about the early part of his life. He'd been a foster kid. One of many who'd gone through Joan Reynolds' house over the years. But he'd never spoken of his life before that. Only of the strong family ties that he'd acquired through that foster family.

He was a good man. That had never been in question. The issue was entirely about her fear of what happened if she tried something and it didn't work. She appreciated him too much as a friend to be willing to risk losing him. And she didn't know whether they could go back to being friends, if she dared to try to change things.

No, it was safer all around to keep the status quo and maintain their friendship. No matter how much she itched to get her hands on him again.

Downstairs, breakfast was being served. She joined a line of guests to load her plate with bacon, eggs, and biscuits before spotting Mick at a table near the window. Based on the convivial air of the crowd, no one seemed particularly upset at the idea of prospectively being stuck another day or two. That made her the odd duck, out of sorts, because she didn't know what to do with herself. Her world involved every hour of every day being allocated to something. She didn't know what to do with free time. She couldn't remember the last time she'd had any.

"What's got you frowning?" Mick's brows rose in concern. "Something wrong back home?"

"No. I spoke to my sister. Everything is good. I'm assured they have everything covered. Though I don't think they'd tell me if it wasn't."

"That bugs you. The not being in control."

"Yeah. I want to know if there are problems."

"Even if you can't do something about them from here?"

She scowled. "You sound like Skylar."

"She's a smart cookie, your baby sister. They'll be fine. I texted with Declan. Derp is doing just fine, and he's perfectly welcome to stay as long as he needs."

So her pooch was taken care of, and her family was shutting her out either way. "So now what?"

He kicked back in his chair with a fresh cup of coffee and a questioning look. "Now what?"

"What do we do all day?"

Those big shoulders twitched. "We play. Haven't you ever played hooky?"

"Of course not." The idea of deliberately cutting class or

work or any other responsibility simply for the sake of having fun was not something that would ever have occurred to her.

With a grin, Mick leaned over and patted her hand. "Stick with me, Padawan. I'm going to teach you my ways. We're gonna have the best snow day ever."

She couldn't help but be drawn to that effervescence. To him. Picking up her own coffee, she met the challenge in his gaze. "Well then, help me, Obi-Wan Kenobi. You're my only hope."

FIVE

Mick eyed the rounded balls of snow stacked almost as tall as Juliette herself. "What should we name him?"

"I don't know. Bob?"

He laughed. "Really?"

"Or maybe Fred? I don't know. I've never made a snowman before."

The idea of it boggled his mind. "You've never made a snowman before?"

Across from him, Juliette smoothed her gloved hands over the snowman's head. "We don't tend to get this kind of snow back home. And on those rare occasions we got a snow day from school, we were always extremely busy at the restaurant because people wanted takeout."

Mick hadn't ever really thought about those businesses that didn't close just because school shut down or there was a holiday. Jade Palace only closed one day a week, and for Thanksgiving and Christmas Day. They were always open, a reliable source of food for those who didn't want to cook or had a kitchen disaster and needed to feed people in a hurry. Given

Juliette's mom's health, that meant Juliette had likely always been there to make sure they could keep providing the service the town had come to count on. Christ, no wonder she had no idea how to take a break.

"Was it different when you were little? Before your parents split?"

Her hands stilled. Something he couldn't read flashed across her face. Nostalgia? The corners of her mouth tipped up a little. "Yeah. Mom was a lot of fun before her illness." A faint look of horror took over, and she rushed to add, "Not that she's not fun now, it's just a lot harder for her. Life takes a lot out of her." Her gaze dropped to the careful insertion of the rocks they'd scrounged for the snowman's face. "She's had more bad days than good lately."

He knew that would tear Juliette up, both as a daughter and as a nurse.

Because he didn't think she'd go for the hug he wanted to give her, Mick kept his attention on the branches he was inserting for arms. "It's hard to watch the people we love struggle. The last years with my grandmother were like that."

"You lived with your grandmother?" There was no mistaking the spark of interest in her tone.

"Yeah. She raised me from about three. My parents dumped me off there and disappeared." It was his turn to jerk his shoulders. "Given the stories I heard about them later, that was probably for the best." He lifted his gaze to Juliette's. "She wasn't a young woman, so I understand what it is to be expected to help out a lot from the time that I was young." It felt vital, somehow, that she see the commonality they shared. As if that might overcome some of the reticence she held. Because Mick didn't think that reluctance toward something more was about him specifically. Not after what she'd shared last night.

She studied him, her eyes full of empathy. "What happened to her? Your grandmother?"

"Same story as a lot of people. She got sick. Cancer. They found it late." And she hadn't told him. Hadn't said a word and had taken every damned thing on herself. Until she couldn't take care of him or herself anymore.

Twitching his shoulders at the memory, Mick smoothed the snow. "When she couldn't take care of me anymore, I went to Joan. She died only a couple months later."

"How old were you?"

"Fourteen." That had been a couple of years before Juliette and her family had come to the Ridge.

"I'm sorry. That's hard. Cancer's a bitch."

"Damn straight. But we had a lot of good years together. I know she loved me, and I was damn lucky to go to Joan when everything was done." His foster mom had been one of the best people he'd ever known, the lynchpin who'd made a family out of the countless misfits in her care, teaching them to rely on each other when so many important people in their worlds had failed them.

"What was your grandmother like?"

Mick smiled to himself, thinking back. "A damned hard worker. She definitely taught me the value of pulling my weight. But she also taught me the value of finding the good in life. Of making fun out of nothing. Which was good, as we were poor as dirt and didn't have much. But I learned that fun is a lot more about mindset than money."

That smile he couldn't stop thinking about curved Juliette's pretty mouth, but it held a rueful edge. "I've certainly benefited from that viewpoint. As you well know, fun isn't something I know much about. Which is pretty sad, I guess."

"There's nothing to be ashamed of in doing what's necessary to take care of your family. But we're still having an intervention. I know this time here away from things is rare for you, so we're going to make the most of it."

Something flickered over her face at that. Fascination? Curiosity? It probably wasn't an interest in the kinds of fun that he'd been dreaming about most of the night. The naked kind that would make good use of that bed they still had to share.

Then her gaze dropped to his lips, and Mick reassessed.

Was it finally time to explore this as a possibility? With her finally away from all of her responsibilities, was this actually an opportunity to see if there was something else here? There was really only one way to find out. He'd just have to tread very, very carefully, and read her signals to make certain he didn't cross any unwanted lines.

Figuring there was no time like the present, he took a step toward her. But before he could say or do anything more, a flash of movement behind her had him reaching out to drag her against his chest, spinning them both so it was him that took the massive snowball.

He flinched as the cold exploded against his back.

Juliette gave a little shriek. "What...?"

"We're under attack!" Mick dragged her over behind a woodpile for some cover, immediately digging his hands into the snow. "We've gotta build an arsenal."

Juliette dared to peek over the top and nearly got a snowball to the face for her trouble. She promptly dropped back down. "We've been ambushed by the Lost Ridge Ramblers." Her voice shook with amusement.

"That'll be a story that nobody else will have. Keep working on ammunition. I'll fire it back." Drawing on his years playing baseball for the Eden's Ridge Wildcats back in high school, he winged a snowball across the yard toward the fiddle player, Issac McLaughlin, who danced out of the way with a laugh.

Was he working alone, or were the rest of his bandmates

out here? A quick scan of the yard showed him Daisy Townsend darting behind a bush with a giggle that rang through the crisp morning air. That was two. There was still Brooke Baxter and Felix Simmons unaccounted for.

Mick scooped up more of the tightly packed snowballs Juliette had hurriedly made and hurled them toward their assailants. They gave back in kind, shouting back taunts.

"Is that the best you've got?"

More guests spilled out of the inn, yelping as they got caught in the crossfire, then running to find their own cover and join in.

Snowballs flew fast and furious, underpinned by joking insults and more laughter. Juliette joined in. She was a pitiful shot, her throws having limited range, but when she managed to hit an unsuspecting guest right in the chest, she crowed with victory, eyes bright.

Those eyes pulled Mick in, inviting him to drown. Before he could give in to insanity, he spotted motion behind her. Felix crept out of the trees, Brooke at his side. Both held snowballs at the ready.

"Our cover's blown. We've gotta make a run for it." He grabbed Juliette's hand and towed her out from behind the woodpile, intending to sprint for the parking lot twenty yards away.

But the depth of the snow hampered their progress, making them sitting ducks.

"Get 'em!"

Juliette shrieked as the first of the barrage hit them. Mick dragged her around, trying to shield her with his body. But he tripped in the thick snow and went sprawling, effectively tackling her into a snowbank. Knowing it was too late for anything else, he curled over her as more snow pelted them both.

Eventually, the sound of laughter moved away, as those still standing went after new targets.

"I think maybe we're safe now," she murmured.

Mick lifted his head and carefully looked around, verifying that fact. "Seems like." He levered himself up far enough he could look into Juliette's face.

Her cheeks were flushed, her eyes sparkling as she reached up to brush the snow from his hair. "You sacrificed yourself for me."

"Seemed the least I could do." And with her hand on him, he no longer felt the snow that had worked its way under his collar and down the back of his shirt.

"My hero."

Her hand lingered on his cheek, and her eyes dropped to his mouth again. That just made him look at her lips, finding them rosy and so very inviting. The pulse of awareness hit him low in the gut as he realized he was stretched out fully over the top of her, one knee pressed into the snow between her thighs.

He ought to move. But toward her or away?

Slowly, carefully, he bent his head, eyes on hers.

Juliette sucked in a breath, her mouth parting just a little, but she didn't push him away. Instead, her fingers curved against his cheek, and...

A snowball hit him right in the side of the face, exploding between them and shattering the moment.

That was it. He was gathering the biggest ball of snow and smashing it right on the head of whoever had just done that. He rolled off Juliette and into a crouch, scanning for the perpetrator.

Daisy Townsend stood at the corner of the inn, hands over her mouth, eyes wide. "Sorry! I was aiming for Felix!"

Beside him, Juliette was scrambling to her feet, expression fierce and mischievous, a snowball already in her hand. "Let's get her."

God, he was crazy for this woman.

"On three..." He counted down, scooping up snow as he did.

Then, with joint battle cries, they launched themselves.

"I'M FREEZING." Juliette wrapped her arms around herself, shaking with wet and cold as she and Mick joined the crowd, stumbling in from the snow battle outside, in response to Lucy's offer of hot chocolate.

Mick nudged her across the main lodge seating area, toward one of the several fireplaces. Like everyone else, they'd left their snow encrusted boots in trays beside the door. But their outer layers were still soaked through from melted snow. Racks had been set up for outerwear along the edges of the room, and blankets were stacked and waiting. The general mood of the crowd was convivial, everyone still laughing and joking after the battle.

Juliette stopped in front of the wide hearth, extending her hands toward the snapping flames inside. Her fingers tingled with little bursts of pain as the warmth began to thaw them.

"We need to get out of these wet layers." Mick immediately peeled off his coat, and Juliette did the same.

The snow had penetrated her sweater underneath, so she immediately began to strip it up and off, but the wet fabric tangled on her arms.

"Here, let me help with that." Mick grabbed the sweater, tugging it off from his greater height. The motion bumped their bodies together. As the fabric untangled from her arms and cleared her head, she looked up into his face and saw a flash of heat, quickly banked.

All the longing she'd felt in that snowbank came flooding

back. He'd been about to kiss her then, and the prospect of it made her breathless now, though he made no move to close the short distance between them. She'd cursed Daisy Townsend six ways from Sunday, because she wanted that kiss. She wanted him to make that move and change things, so she didn't have to.

Coward.

She didn't deny it. But she wasn't in the habit of being brave for herself. Only for her family. And that was probably why she had very little that was only hers. The apartment she'd moved into after nursing school, because she had to have somewhere she could let the walls down and feel all the things it wasn't safe to feel anywhere else. Derp. Because he gave her joy, even if he did require a lot more care than a younger, fitter dog. Those were the only things she'd allowed herself.

But here, in this holiday-themed inn, so far from her everyday, she found she wanted something else for herself. Damn her sister for putting the idea into her head. Except, could she really blame Skylar as the reason she'd been imagining Mick naked? This was hardly the first time. But it was the first time she hadn't been able to shut that train of thought down with reiterations of all the practical reasons it was a bad idea.

It was reckless thinking. Counter to all her good intentions to be satisfied with his friendship alone. But that didn't change the want.

Not taking his eyes off hers, Mick reached past her to drape her sweater on the nearest rack. Juliette's belly jittered under that long, interested gaze. God, how long had it been since she'd felt real mutual attraction? Or more properly, how long had it been since she'd *let* herself feel it? More years than she cared to count. Now that the leash was off, she wasn't sure she could wrestle it back into a cage.

She wasn't sure she wanted to.

Lips curved, eyes laughing with the characteristic joy she

loved, Mick stripped his own fleece pullover off and added it to the rack. Then he grabbed one of the blankets, shaking it open and draping it around her, using the ends to pull her closer. Near enough she could feel the warmth of him even more than she could feel the heat of the fire at her back.

"Better?" She felt the vibration of the word through her palms where they rested on his chest, and she had to fight not to explore the contours of the lean muscles there. That didn't stop her brain from imagining what it would be like to run her fingers over his bare skin. To follow them with her lips.

A little afraid of what might come out of her mouth if she spoke, Juliette just nodded. They were friends. They hugged. He was a guy who believed in physical affection. But this was different. And maybe he was testing them both to explore the edges of this shift that was happening between them.

"Hot chocolate?"

At the sound of Lucy's voice, they both turned. The older woman held a tray full of steaming mismatched mugs. Her smile winked as she held it out. "Extra marshmallows."

"That is the law of hot cocoa." Mick released one side of the blanket as he reached for a mug.

Juliette snagged another. "Thanks. This is great." She could already feel the heat of the drink soaking into her palm.

The proprietress moved on to other guests.

"Looks like the rest of the blankets are gone. We're gonna have to share," Mick announced.

She fixed him with a mock side eye. "Oh, the horror." Okay, as an opening volley of flirtation, it wasn't the best. But Mick grinned and took the other side of the blanket, tugging it around his shoulders before urging her to sit on the hearth behind them.

It wasn't a huge blanket, so they were pressed leg to leg, shoulder to shoulder. He seemed to put off every bit as much heat as the fire. Drawn in by it, for more than one reason, she looped her arm through his and tipped her head to his shoulder.

"How are you so warm? I feel like a human popsicle. You're a furnace."

"Bigger body mass retains heat better."

"Is that actually true?"

"No idea, but it sounds true. I've always run hot."

She cuddled a little closer. "Excuse me while I take shameless advantage."

"You can take advantage of me anytime." He uttered the invitation in the same easy, amused tone he seemed to use all the time, but the weight of his meaning settled over her like a warm, weighted blanket.

He was letting her run this show. If things were going to change, it would be on her to set the pace and extent. That was both comfort and stress. She didn't know how to do this anymore. Didn't know how to flirt or seduce.

So she didn't attempt either, instead settling her head against his shoulder with a sigh. "This is nice."

After a moment, she felt the barest brush of his lips against her temple. "Yeah, it is. Not bad for your first snow day?"

"Not bad at all."

Anticipation shimmered inside her, a hope that she hardly dared analyze. She'd spent so long trying not to look at him with any possibility, but the past couple of days had changed things. He made her want. Not just the physical—although, yes, that too—but everything that he could offer. He wasn't like her ex or her father. He was a man who sought to help, to make things easier. This trip was proof enough of that. Yet she was still afraid. Not that he'd be indifferent or that they'd crash and burn. She was terrified that this time-out-of-time wouldn't be something she could take home. She had to decide whether to take the risk or let this opportunity pass.

SIX

Juliette was officially flirting with him. It had taken a while for Mick to decide for sure that he was reading the situation correctly, but the cuddling after they'd thawed out was the clincher. They were friends who hugged. They were not friends who snuggled or held hands. They'd been doing both all afternoon as the guests turned to a massive board game tournament for entertainment. Turned out, Juliette had a vicious competitive streak and was a ruthless Monopoly baron. She'd played everybody else under the table, and he'd had a hell of a time watching her do it.

After dinner, they'd all congregated in the main lodge for Christmas carols, led by the Lost Ridge Ramblers. Informal and acoustic, everyone felt free to join in with anything they knew. Though much, much larger, it reminded Mick of some of the Christmases with Joan and all his various foster siblings. There'd always been someone with musical talent to play an instrument and lead them. Those were some of his fondest memories. As Juliette sang in a quiet alto beside him, her fingers curled with his, this one was climbing the charts.

Things were changing between them, and it was time to give that a little nudge. Chances were, they'd be going home tomorrow, and this window of opportunity might close. He had no idea if she'd revert to form when thrust back into her normal life, and he might not get another shot. So, when the informal concert concluded and everybody split up, peeling off to their rooms or into the pub for one last drink for the night, he tugged Juliette to her feet.

"Want to go for a little walk before bed?"

"Sure."

They donned all the outerwear that had dried by the fire over the course of the afternoon and stepped out into the cold. The mass of snow hadn't melted, but there hadn't been any additional precipitation. At some point in the day, a few paths had been shoveled around the inn's perimeter. Keeping her hand in his, he tugged her onto the path leading toward the front of the building.

When Juliette said nothing, he gently bumped her shoulder with his. "Penny for your thoughts."

"I was just thinking how peaceful it is here. Even being snowed in with all of these people, being locked away from the normal world has been really nice." She glanced up at him, and he could just see the blush of her cheeks in the moonlight. "Being trapped here with you has been really nice. I'm glad you asked me along."

Heart pounding, he kept his tone easy. "Me too."

They'd almost reached their destination. He'd spotted the little gazebo earlier in the day and had filed it away for just such an opportunity. The steps hadn't been cleared, so he carefully helped her navigate the piles of snow to the center.

Juliette pulled out her phone and switched on the flashlight, shining it around. "Looks like there are fairy lights. I bet this is really cute when the power's on."

Mick shone his own flashlight above their heads. "I think Lucy was going more for romantic than cute." He pointed to the mistletoe that had been mounted to the rafters. Hardly daring to breathe, he waited to see what her reaction would be, if she'd step away or blush or otherwise balk at the implication.

But she did none of that. A little smile quirked the corners of her mouth, prompting a matching crease at the edges of her eyes as she turned off the light and tucked the phone away. "Is that why you wanted to go for a walk?"

Wanting his hands free, he put his own phone away. "Would it be a problem if it was?" This was as open as he'd ever been about his interest in her beyond friendship.

Slowly, she shook her head.

Sending up a thousand prayers of thanks, Mick stepped closer, pulling her against him. "Well, then." Gently, he stroked the hair back from her face. "I've wanted to do this for a really long time." He waited to see how that admission landed.

"Really?" In the dark, he couldn't really see her face clearly, but there was no mistaking the pleasure in her tone.

"Yeah. But I never wanted to push you. You're one of my best friends, and if we weren't on the same page, I didn't want to screw something up."

For a long moment, she stayed silent. "It was never that we weren't on the same page. It was that I never thought I had enough to offer you."

The confession made his heart twist. This woman. God. She was spread so thin, and he wanted to do whatever he could to help with that.

Brushing his thumb along the arch of her cheek, he murmured, "Isn't that for me to decide?"

"I'm starting to think it is." She pressed closer, her hands curling into his coat.

He couldn't see her eyes, but he felt a yearning in her that matched his own. That same pulse that had overtaken them in the snowbank this morning began to thrum through him, and when he pulled her even closer, she didn't fight it. His hand skimmed along the velvety soft skin of her cheek, into the silk of her hair.

"Juliette."

At the low rasp of his voice, she sighed, lifting her face toward his. He lowered his head slowly, giving her all the time in the world to pull back. Instead, she rose to her toes and met his mouth with hers.

Her lips were soft. Mick took his time exploring them in a devastatingly slow kiss that made his heart thunder. He felt an echo of that pulse where his palm brushed her throat. At the first questioning touch of his tongue, she opened for him, and damn if that surrender didn't make him want more. As the taste of her flooded into him, he shuddered. All the carefully erected walls he'd put into place to keep himself under control simply collapsed, leaving him with nothing but need.

He'd known this would be here. Had known the wanting would run deep. But he hadn't been sure she'd share it. When he drew her closer still, angling for a deeper taste, she came willingly, sliding her hands up his chest, over his shoulders to pull him even closer. A possessive growl rumbled his chest against hers, and she whimpered, sagging against him as if her knees had gone weak.

Mick wanted more. Wanted to strip her bare and feast on that gloriously soft skin, to taste that compact, capable body. To make her mindless with pleasure, then lose himself in her.

But he pulled himself back. This was already a lot. More than he'd expected. He wouldn't push her too far, too fast.

Juliette was breathing hard as she slid down his body, back to her feet. He was pretty sure she'd have kept going to sink right down to the gazebo floor if he hadn't had hold of her.

Her voice shook a little as she murmured, "Well then."

With a huff of laughter, he dropped his brow to hers. "So, that happened."

"Yeah."

"Is it going to happen again?"

"God, I hope so."

"Thank God." Mick blew out a breath and lifted her hand to his lips for a kiss. "Let's go inside. It's freezing out here."

"I feel like there are now more interesting ways to warm up."

Heart thumping, he wrapped his arms around her. "I definitely like the way you think."

NERVES DANCED along Juliette's skin as they made their way inside and upstairs to their room. Mick's kiss had electrified every inch of her, including quite a few that hadn't seen attention from anyone but her in far longer than she cared to remember. He made her want in ways she always denied herself. But tonight was likely their last here at the inn. Surely the roads would be cleared by tomorrow and they'd be making their way back home. Back to all the responsibilities she'd escaped for these few blessed days.

What if this was her last opportunity to take something purely for herself before life intruded again? She didn't want to waste it.

So when they stepped into their room and he shut the door behind them, she didn't give herself a chance to rethink it. "Mick?"

"Hmm?"

With a bracing breath, Juliette turned to face him. "Will you take me to bed?"

If some part of her was mortified by having baldly blurted her request of him, it was drowned out by the instant flare of heat that brightened his eyes to jade. He wanted her. She'd cling to that and let the rest go.

His throat worked. "That's a big step. We should probably talk about it."

Something that might have been panic added to the jitters in her belly. She shook her head. "I don't want to talk. I don't want to think. If I stop, I'll talk myself out of it like I talk myself out of every single thing for myself for the last forever." She knew her eyes mirrored the heat in his as she looked up at him. "Please. I don't want to talk myself out of this with you."

If he tried to be sensible and rational, she might just die of embarrassment.

Instead, he stepped into her, sliding his hands into her hair and cradling her head. "You don't want to think?"

The rumble of his voice stroked along her skin like a caress. Shuddering, she shook her head again.

Mick smiled. "Challenge accepted."

He took her mouth in a slow, devouring kiss that stole her breath and banished any lingering trepidation. Juliette reached for him, gripping his narrow hips and pulling him closer, close enough to feel the strain of his erection against her belly. Her inner muscles tightened in anticipation, even as he began to back her toward the bed, taking that marvelous mouth on a tour down her throat.

"You have no idea how much I've wanted this. Wanted you."

Breathless, delighted, she could only gasp, "Really?"

His hands efficiently stripped off her coat. "Years."

Eyes wide, her own hands froze as she stared up at him.

Those broad shoulders flexed in a shrug, and he flashed a rueful smile as he tugged her sweater and T-shirt over her head.

"I never would have forced the issue. But if you don't mind, I intend to take my time about this." He punctuated his point by bending to place a kiss just above the valley of her breasts, his beard stubble scraping gently against her skin.

Juliette's voice wheezed out. "No, I don't mind slow."

With a flick of his fingers, he unfastened her bra and drew it away, leaving her chest bare to his gaze. "Lovely."

He cupped her breasts in those deliciously work-roughened hands and circled his thumbs around her nipples. They pearled at his touch, and her knees went weak. Then he sucked one taut bud into his mouth and sensation exploded through her. She moaned, her hands diving into his hair, holding him to her as he suckled. She didn't even realize he'd unzipped her jeans until the warmth of his hand slid between her legs. He had only to part her folds, his finger dipping into the wetness there and circling her clit to send her flying.

By the time she came down from the whiplash of climax, she was spread out on the bed, and he'd managed to divest her of the rest of her clothes. Well, he was nothing if not efficient.

His big hand curved around the dip of her waist. "Okay? Not too cold?"

Juliette blinked at him. "What's temperature?"

Mick grinned and kissed her again, clouding her mind and stoking fresh embers of arousal as he worked his way down her torso and lower, lingering at the flare of her hips and on each quivering thigh. Then he settled between her legs and absolutely delivered on his promise to make her mindless and unable to speak. Though he hadn't said a word about not making her scream.

Boneless and gasping, she peered down the length of her body to find him wearing a smug, self-satisfied smile. Seeing him there, in that incredibly intimate position, her heart rolled over. Because she'd trusted him with her body. Maybe she could trust him with more. Beyond the weekend.

"Doing okay up there?"

She dropped her head back to the pillow. "I may be half dead, but I'm definitely a whole lot better than okay."

"We can stop."

She looked down again in time to catch the devilish glint in his eyes and gave a little tug on his hair. "Don't you dare." She paused as an iota of sense returned. "Unless you don't have a condom?"

He pressed a kiss to the inside of her thigh. "Wait right here."

He slid off the bed and rushed into the bathroom. She heard him rustling around, digging through his Dopp kit, then the sound of running water as he quickly brushed his teeth. God bless him. Less than a minute later, he returned and began stripping his own clothes.

Having regained some muscle control, she straightened and held up her hand. "Wait."

Mick froze, arms crossed, shirt halfway up his torso.

Juliette scooted off the bed and reached for him. "Let me."

That grin came back as she tugged off his T-shirt and explored the chest she'd been dreaming about, getting a little quid pro quo by tonguing his nipples until he shuddered. His heart thundered beneath her palm. The heavy beat of it filled her with a surge of feminine power. She'd done that. And she intended to do more.

Reaching for his belt, she unbuckled it, slowly drawing the leather free. Enjoying the anticipation, she took her own time lowering the zipper and slowly pushing his jeans down his legs, getting a palmful of his delightfully muscular ass in the process. Free of the jeans, his erection already tented his black boxer briefs. Needing to see him, she tugged those down, too, until he stood naked before her.

He was beautiful. All long lean muscles. The kind built from hard labor instead of the gym. A smattering of dark hair dusted his chest, narrowing to a happy trail leading down to the proud jut of his cock. God, she wanted him inside her. Wanted to feel the girth of him sliding into her heat, filling up all those empty places she pretended not to feel.

Juliette rose to kiss him again, wrapping her arms around his neck as their bodies pressed together, front to front. His hands skated down her spine, over the globes of her butt, to grip her under the thighs and lift. It was the most natural thing in the world to wrap her legs around his waist. Without breaking the kiss, he sank back onto the bed so she splayed across his lap. His erection nestled between her thighs, and she squirmed a little, stroking the length of him through her wetness as she patted around on the duvet for the condom he'd dropped there.

With a little growl, his fingers dug into her hips, stilling the motion. "You're gonna want to stop that unless you want this over before it's started."

"Can't have that." With a little cry of triumph, she held up the foil packet.

He let her do the honors of rolling it on. Then she pushed him back, rising over him. He stared up at her as if she were a goddess. That look was power and intoxication. Her ex had never made her feel like this.

The intrusive thought made her pause. Maybe he'd rather be the one in control. "Is this okay?"

"Anything is okay. We can do this however you like."

Reassured, she braced her hands on either side of his head and bent to kiss him as she lowered her hips, slowly taking him inside her, inch by slow inch. They both moaned. The blunt intrusion of him felt absolutely delicious. His hands curled around her hips, but he didn't rush, didn't try to take over. He simply held on as she sank onto him fully.

Groaning her name, Mick slid that big hand into her hair and around to cup her nape. God, she loved when he did that. It made her feel wanted and safe. Everything about him made her feel taken care of.

He pulled her down far enough to take her mouth again, and she began to move, rising ever so slowly before sinking back down again and again. Their rhythm was slow, an inexorable build toward what she knew would be a magnificent detonation. Beneath her, he trembled with the effort to hold back. She was already so very close, so she rolled, taking him with her, until his big body was ranged over hers.

With a quick nip at his mouth, she urged, "Harder."

He took her at her word, whipping his hips in a pistoning motion that drove him deeper, striking at a spot inside her that was oh, so perfect.

Juliette's head fell back against the pillow. "More!"

Shifting, he pressed one of her knees back, opening her wider so he could drive even deeper. So deep, she didn't think she'd ever stop feeling him inside her. And she didn't want to. She didn't want this to ever stop.

He drove her impossibly higher, until she finally shattered on a cry. And as her body clamped around him, he called out her name and spilled inside her.

SEVEN

Mick snapped awake, uncertain what had woken him. The room was dark, and a very warm, very naked Juliette was wrapped around him, sleeping. Everything was fine. Better than fine. He ought to go back to sleep. But something continued to niggle, so he held still, listening, trying to identify what had disturbed him.

Apparently, his lingering tension woke his lovely bedmate.

"Wha's wrong?" Her voice was slurred with sleep, and no wonder.

Neither of them had gotten too much sleep tonight. Last night? What time was it?

Mick settled back against his pillow, tucking her closer. "I don't know. Something's different."

Her hand skimmed down his naked flank, and she nuzzled his throat. "I thought we'd already established what that was."

His low chuckle turned into a moan as her hand slid lower. "I meant besides that."

He shouldn't have had any energy left at all. But he felt

himself stir yet again between beneath her questing fingers. He certainly wasn't going to turn down another opportunity to make love to this woman. He rolled over, pinning her beneath him, delighting at the automatic spread of her legs to welcome him.

And he caught sight of the glow outside the window.

"The power's back on."

Juliette's hands stilled. "Are you sure?"

"The exterior lights are on. Those weren't running on the generators. They must've finally gotten the lines fixed sometime in the middle of the night."

She hesitated, and he wished he could read her expression in the dark.

"I guess that means we're going home today."

He didn't want this weekend to end. That was the only excuse he had for why he had to bring up the elephant in the room right now, while he was all but inside her. "Is this only going to be for this weekend or is this going to be a change we take home?"

Juliette stretched beneath him, and suddenly the bedside light switched on, bathing the room in a dim glow. She lay back down, eyes searching his face. "You'd really be okay if this was just for the weekend?"

Her expression was serious, and he wished he knew what she was looking for. But all he could give her was the absolute truth.

"I mean, I would prefer this remain a permanent change, but I understand you feel like your life is complicated." He brushed the hair tenderly back from her face. "I don't want to be another complication. I only ever want to make things better for you."

Something in her lovely dark eyes softened, and she

reached up to frame his face in her palms, leaning up far enough to brush her lips to his. "I don't think I can go back to not having this."

Mick closed his eyes and almost collapsed on her in relief. "Thank God." He'd gotten behind her walls this weekend, and he didn't want to go back to being on the outside.

Juliette eased back down to the pillows, staring up at him in a sort of wonder. "I still can't quite believe you want me."

Now that the danger was past, Mick let some of his usual humor leak back out. "I think the indisputable evidence of that fact is waiting for another round."

She arched her hips against him in invitation. "I'm for that." She reached toward the bedside table for the strip of condoms. "I've been meaning to ask... Are you just a well-prepared Boy Scout? Or were you being optimistic when you packed for this weekend?"

He bit off his chuckle as she sheathed him again, rolling down the condom and giving his cock a squeeze. "They were left over from Kendrick's bachelor party. A pseudo gag gift I got all the groomsmen. I just never took them out of my Dopp kit." And thank God for it, as they'd put quite a dent in the strip last night.

"How fortunate for us both." And she pulled him down to her, into her.

Her wet heat fisted around him, a welcome he'd never tire of. They made love slowly, lazily. As if they had all the time in the world. As if the roads wouldn't be open today and taking them back to normal life. They both wanted to linger here, soaking up as much pleasure as possible before life interrupted again.

Afterward, they retreated to the bathroom to clean up, taking advantage of a long, blissfully hot shower, where they had each other again, and Juliette proved he wasn't the only one who could make someone scream.

It was well and truly dawn by the time they'd finished and made it to fully dressed. Mick was pretty sure everyone who saw him would know he'd gotten laid repeatedly last night. He was too damn happy to care. His best friend, the woman he'd been crazy about for years, was finally his in every way that mattered. What the hell did he have to complain about?

The scent of coffee lured them into the pub, where Lucy was prepping the buffet for breakfast. Only a handful of other guests were scattered around the room.

The older woman beamed at them as they approached. "Good morning! Don't you two look all fine and relaxed this morning. Good night's sleep?"

Mick didn't miss the twitch of Lucy's lips, but he didn't bat an eye. "The best. I saw the power was back."

"Yes. Restored sometime last night. I got word from the road crews that they'll be working on plowing this section of the county today, but given we're the only thing out here and are well off the beaten path, they warned me we're toward the end of the route. We still may not be able to get out of here until tomorrow."

Mick glanced reflexively at Juliette and found a smile curving that kiss-pinkened mouth. Another day here, away from everything waiting at home? Oh, darn.

Lucy was still talking. "I know quite a few folks are trying to make arrangements to change their flights."

Juliette snuggled up against his side. "That won't be a problem for us. We drove over from Tennessee. But is there anything we can do to help out? I know you certainly weren't planning on having this many guests for this long."

"Oh, we're making it just fine. Thank you, dearie. Y'all get yourselves a good hearty breakfast. Gotta fuel up for... whatever you decide to do with your day."

Juliette tucked her flaming face against his shoulder, but Mick couldn't do anything but grin as he reached for a plate. "Carb loading it is."

JULIETTE LET herself into the quiet of her apartment and dropped her bag. No scrambling, snorting pup waiting. Derp was still with Mick's brother, Declan. Even though everything was exactly as she'd left it, the place felt empty and strange. Different.

Maybe it wasn't her apartment that was different, but her. She was no longer the same woman who'd left here. No longer an island.

The other half of that metaphorical island stepped up behind her, wrapping his arms around her waist and pressing a kiss to the juncture of her neck and shoulder. "Sad to be home?"

Juliette leaned back against Mick, soaking in the comfort of his presence as she sighed. "Yeah. But we couldn't stay gone forever. I need to go check in with my mom and the restaurant." She turned, wrapping her arms around him and tipping her face up to look into those glinting green eyes. "What about you?"

"I've got to go check in with the garage. See what Willie needs me to do. He wasn't expecting me to be gone this long. I'll be arranging some shift swaps with folks to make it up for those who covered me."

They both had responsibilities they couldn't ignore. She'd known this was coming, and she worried what it meant for them. Would they actually manage to make this thing work for real?

As if reading her mind, he tightened his hold. "Shall we make plans to get together later?"

The delicious ache of a body well used reminded her of that morning, their last frantic time together before wishing the Merry Falls Inn and Lucy goodbye and getting on the road. "Didn't get enough of me this weekend?"

"Never." He flashed his grin. "Though I was thinking something more like dinner. Much as I enjoy spending time in bed with you, we've gotta figure out the rest of this whole us thing."

She sighed again, resting her chin against his chest, face tipped up to his. "I like the sound of that. Us."

Mick kissed the tip of her nose. "Go do what you've gotta do. We'll figure out what we're doing later on tonight. And don't worry about Derp. I'll get him on my way home."

That was something off her list, and she was grateful, though she'd missed her pooch something fierce. "Thanks. I'll think of something to take over as a thank you to his family later."

"I can attest that they all have a special fondness for oatmeal chocolate chip cookies."

"Noted." She needed groceries anyway. She could pick up the ingredients whenever she made it to Garden of Eden.

After another long lingering kiss, Mick left her and went next door to drop his own bag off.

As she preferred, Juliet headed down the street on foot. Maybe it was because she'd just spent four days in an inn devoted to Christmas spirit, but she actually noticed the decorations decking out downtown Eden's Ridge. Twinkling white lights were strung between the old-fashioned lampposts that lined the street. Colorful storefronts were adorned with wreaths made of evergreen boughs, red velvet bows, and pinecones—a product of a Boy Scout fundraiser, she knew. She'd bought one for Jade Palace. The aroma of cinnamon and pine wafted from the door of Moonbeams and Sweet Dreams, the gift shop and florist. Its front display was full of nutcrackers, wooden rocking horses, and other nostalgic decorations amidst its holiday wares. Carols played over hidden speakers as, up and down the street, the holiday hustle and bustle carried on with people dashing in and out of the shops, arms laden with gifts and holiday treats.

Juliette felt downright cheerful as she navigated around them. Her cheeks ached from smiling, and she wondered how many people would give thought to why.

I took my best friend as my lover, and it might be the best decision I ever made.

But her smile faded when she reached Jade Palace. The windows were dark. The neon sign off. A paper was taped to the inside of the door. *Closed until further notice by order of The Health Department.*

Dread dropped into her stomach like a ball of lead.

No, oh no. What the hell happened?

Juliette hurried around the corner to the steps that led up to the apartment. She found it locked and used her key to let herself inside. The space was absolutely frigid. There was no sign of Skylar or her mother.

Fresh worry wiped away all the lingering warmth she'd felt from her weekend away with Mick.

Where were they? What had happened?

She whipped out her phone, dialing her sister's number.

Skylar answered on the first ring. "Hey, sis. How was your weekend?"

Juliette ignored the cheerful question, getting straight to

the heart of the matter. "Where are you? Is Mom okay? What happened at the restaurant?"

There was a long pause. "Mom's fine. We're at Tiny's."

"Why are you at Tiny's?"

"Well, the gas to the building has been shut off. So we don't have any heat."

The gas? Had there been a leak? No, if the restaurant was closed by the health department, this wasn't some arbitrary thing.

An ache began building at Juliette's temples. She bent her head, rubbing at the tension. "Why didn't you go to my place?"

"We couldn't find the spare key, and we didn't want to bug you to find out where it was. Tiny offered."

Guilt dug its talons into Juliette's chest. Throat thick, she managed, "What happened with the health department?"

Skylar didn't immediately answer. The longer the silence went on, the more anxiety tightened Juliette's ribcage.

"I think you should talk to Mom about that."

Juliette was already moving. "I'm on my way. Don't go anywhere."

Tiny lived further than she wanted to walk, so she had to rush back to her apartment to pick up her car. By the time she'd made the short drive to Tiny's house, she'd driven herself half mad with questions. Knowing that losing her temper would help nothing, she took several long moments to attempt to compose herself before she got out of the car. That tattered composure disintegrated as she strode up the walk, when the door opened and Tiny's broad frame filled the space. "Where's my mother?"

Without question, the big man backed up, letting her inside. "In the living room." He laid a big hand on her shoulder as she stepped inside. "She's okay."

But Juliette needed to see for herself. She moved straight

through and found her mother curled up at one end of a man-sized sofa, a blanket draped over her lap. She looked so tiny and frail.

Drawing on years of iron control, Juliette managed to keep her voice level. "Mom. What happened with the health department?"

Sue Ellen smiled. "Welcome back! How was your weekend away, sweetheart?"

The last thing Juliette wanted to talk about was Mick. "Don't change the subject, Mom. What happened with the health department?"

Her mother's face clouded, brows drawing together in irritation. "That horrible man came by for a surprise inspection."

'That horrible man' was Ronnie Guthrie, the county health inspector. He and Sue Ellen had never gotten along, so Juliette always made an effort to be present whenever inspections happened, to run interference.

And she hadn't been here, because she'd been playing hooky with Mick. "What did he find?"

Tiny was the one who answered. "He declared the stove is unusable. Which is bunk, since you know it's been working fine. But you know how the door doesn't quite close on the oven. He decided that was too big a risk of a gas leak. Your mama tried to reason with him."

Translation: Sue Ellen had argued with him about it.

"Anyway, he wouldn't allow us to simply shut down the gas line to the stove. He had the gas company shut off gas to the entire building, so there was no heat in the apartment. That's why I brought them here."

"Thank you," Juliette managed.

At least someone had been here to help. But God, it should have been her. She should have been here to take care of this. She could've handled Guthrie with diplomacy, maybe been able to at least convince him to cut the gas line off to the kitchen. Maybe even assured him that they had a new stove on order and this one just needed to hold out a little longer. Even though that would've been a complete lie. She'd have found a way to make it happen.

Instead, the first time in years she'd done something purely for herself, everything had fallen apart. Her family's livelihood had been shut down, and they wouldn't be able to get it up and running again until they had a new stove and could get an inspection scheduled.

She should never have left. She knew better. She knew she was the one holding everything together. This was proof enough of that. The moment she'd left town, everything had unraveled.

"Enough about the restaurant. We'll get it sorted. Tell us about your trip," Sue Ellen insisted.

"Yeah. How are things with you and Mick?" Skylar asked.

"That's the last thing we should be talking about right now." And after today, there wouldn't be anything to talk about. "We have to get the restaurant back open. I'm going to go back by the apartment to pick up the books and figure out where we can find the money."

Juliette had no clue how they were going to afford a new stove. The cost was so astronomically out of reach. That was the whole reason they hadn't replaced the unit yet to begin with. But they had to figure something out because every day that Jade Palace stayed closed was a significant chunk of lost revenue that they couldn't afford.

"Really, honey, it's going to be fine," Sue Ellen said.

But it wouldn't. This was why they needed her. Because she was the only one who thought about the long-term and the practical. The only one who realized that life didn't just magically work out because you wished it.

Tears burned the backs of her eyes, a fresh grief she wouldn't give voice to. Instead, she said goodbye and walked out before she could lose her shit.

Welcome back to the real world, Juliette, where nothing revolves around you.

EIGHT

"Put me down for plus three to the family Christmas dinner."

At the excited squee that came over the line, Mick winced and jerked the phone away from his ear.

"I knew it," Ari crowed. "I knew a weekend away with you and Juliette was going to work!"

He frowned at the phone. "What do you mean you knew? How did you even know I got the tickets from Kendrick and Erin?"

Ari scoffed. "As if they were on their own. Don't question the matchmaker. I assume the other two are going to be Juliette's mom and sister?"

Deciding he didn't really want to know *what* or *who* might have been involved in orchestrating his weekend, he focused on what she'd asked. "Well, I don't know for sure. I haven't asked her yet. But I wouldn't want to take her away from her family for Christmas, so I figure it's better to plan for a yes and back off, than not plan and there be a shortage of food."

"You know there's going to be enough food to feed an army.

No one at The Misfit Inn ever goes hungry. I'll put you down. Keep us posted."

"I'll do that." Mick hesitated. "And whatever you had to do with this whole situation, thanks."

Ari made a kissing noise. "You're welcome."

Mick was still laughing as he hung up.

He'd ended up spending the rest of the afternoon at the garage, helping out with some last-minute projects to see that they were completed in time for the holiday. He'd have more hours to make up after Christmas, but for now, he was off for another few days.

Feeling cheerful, he headed to Declan's to pick up Derp.

His brother met him at the door, a broad grin stretching his face. "Well, well, look who finally came home." Declan's gaze skimmed over him, and his eyes twinkled with glee. "I'd say the weekend was a success."

Mick stepped into the renovated Victorian. "Don't you start. I just got off the phone with Ari. She's claiming credit for the whole thing."

"That's on brand. At least you only had one teenager inter-fering in your love life. I got two."

Declan's daughter, Scarlett, bounced down the stairs. "And you're still thanking me."

"Yes, I am. Why don't you go gather up Derp's stuff? I'm sure Mick is eager to get home." Declan said this last with a suggestive waggle of his eyebrows.

In truth, Mick's entire body ached. But he was looking forward to seeing Juliette again over dinner so they could talk about their respective days. He'd been wondering how things went for her family while she was out of town.

Seeing no sign of Declan's wife, Livia, Mick asked, "Where's your better half?"

"Still up at the shop. At Your Leisure has been jumping with last-minute holiday shoppers, so they've been open late."

The bookstore and wine bar had opened earlier in the year to much fanfare and success. Mick knew Juliette enjoyed popping in from time to time, when she was able. Maybe he'd get her a gift card there for Christmas.

Scarlett returned, trailed by Hagrid and Derp. She handed over the dog bed and bag of toys and supplies. "He had a blast. So did the rest of us."

Declan eyed his daughter. "Don't be thinking that's a weight in favor of getting another puppy. One is enough."

Hagrid and Derp turned twin soulful looks his way.

"Nope. No. I'm immune. Mick, take him away."

Laughing as his brother carefully didn't meet the dogs' gazes, he scooped up Derp and headed out the door.

The dog rode in his lap for the short drive back to the apartment. Juliette's car was in the back. He hoped that meant she was home, though he knew she regularly preferred to walk when she could. Tucking the chubby furball under his arm, he tossed the bag of stuff over his shoulders and grabbed the dog bed with his free hand. He hauled the lot of it upstairs, juggling it so he could unlock the door and let himself inside. He went straight to Juliette's apartment and knocked.

After a few long moments, the door swung open, and Mick felt his bubble of happiness burst. Juliette's face was white with strain, and there were fresh brackets of worry around her mouth and eyes.

"What's wrong?"

Without meeting his gaze, she reached for the dog, lowering her head to rub her cheek against his fur in an unmistakable bid for comfort. Saying nothing, she turned and moved further into the apartment.

More than a little worried, Mick followed her inside. He

put Derp's stuff down and turned to face her. "Juliette, honey, what is it?"

"I shouldn't have left."

He couldn't make sense of the rasp in her voice. "What are you talking about? Everything was taken care of." He'd made sure of it. Hadn't he?

The look she shot him was full of defeat. "You tried to cover everything, but there was no way you could've accounted for this."

Seriously worried now, Mick stepped into her, wrapping her and Derp in a hug. "Talk to me. What happened?"

She sucked in a shuddering breath. "The restaurant is closed."

Whatever he'd expected, it wasn't that. "Closed? Why?"

"By order of the health inspector, until further notice." Her tone was flat. A dry recitation of fact that did nothing to mask the devastation beneath.

"The health department? But I've seen that kitchen. It's immaculate."

"It wasn't a cleanliness violation. Although the notice says nothing about that, so probably a lot of town will think that's what it is. When we do get back open, we'll probably lose business for a while."

Filing that under things to address later, Mick pressed, "If not that kind of violation, what was the issue? "

Juliette sighed, and he saw the weight of the world bowing her shoulders again. "The oven was declared unusable. The health inspector was concerned about a gas leak, so he shut off the gas to the entire building, instead of simply the one appliance. Mom and Skylar have been staying with Tiny, because there's no heat in the apartment."

Oh shit. One problem at a time. "What's wrong with the stove?"

She shook her head. "I don't know exactly. The door doesn't shut quite right. There may have been something else. It's been on its last leg for a long time, but we just haven't been able to afford to replace it. But with this? We don't have a choice. And I don't see how we're going to afford a new unit with how our finances are running."

Mick's brain was already spinning. "Maybe you don't need a brand-new one. Aren't there used restaurant supply stores?"

"That would be the best-case scenario, but so far, I haven't had any luck finding one that has what we need, in a size that will fit. There may be others, but with the holiday this week, a lot of the suppliers are closed. It's a problem." Her chin wobbled, and those eyes filled with tears. "I don't know what we're going to do. The longer we're closed, the less likely we are to be able to afford what we need to get up and running again. It's a catch twenty-two."

Mick pulled her in tighter, close enough that the dog grumbled in complaint. "It's going to be okay." He didn't know how, but he would find a way to make it so, because he couldn't stand to see her struggling like this.

Juliette lifted shimmering eyes to his, a resolute look on her lovely face. "It's not going to be okay, Mick."

And he knew. Even before she opened her mouth to say the words, he understood that this had shattered her confidence in the idea that she could take anything for herself. Her family and their welfare would always come first, and she didn't think she should even be on the list.

"I can't do this. I was right. I have way too much responsibility on my shoulders, and I can't afford any more distractions. You are a wonderful, glorious distraction. This weekend was amazing. But it's all I can give you. I have nothing left." The tears she'd struggled to hold back slipped down her cheeks. She dashed them away with her free hand before he could. "I'm sorry."

Frustration shimmered through him. She claimed she wanted to spare him, but all she was doing was shutting him out. Exactly as his grandmother had. This was exactly what he been afraid of. Exactly what he'd always known he'd have to fight. She was so bound by the habit of being the only one to take care of things for her family, and he didn't exactly know how to combat that.

But by damn, he was going to find a way, because he wasn't willing to give her up this easily. He didn't want to be on the outside. He wanted to be there, by her side, helping her find a way.

Still, he understood that arguing with her about it right now wouldn't get him anywhere. She was too raw, too vulnerable. She felt too underwater to even think about entertaining the idea of a permanent them. So he'd do what she asked and back off.

For now.

Pressing a kiss to her brow, he forced himself to step back, letting her go, even though it was the absolute last thing he wanted to do. "You know where I'll be if you change your mind. Let me know if there's anything I can do to help."

Her throat worked as she swallowed, and for a moment he wondered if she'd waver. But finally, she nodded.

As it seemed there was nothing more to say, Mick left her there, regretting every step and cursing stubborn women who didn't know how to let anyone take some of the load.

The moment he'd made it down the hall and into his own apartment, he pulled out his phone and made a call.

He wasn't giving her up without a fight.

JULIETTE HADN'T SLEPT. She'd spent most of the night combing through the books for Jade Palace. No matter which way she sliced, diced, and crunched the numbers, there was no conceivable way they could afford an entirely new stove. Not without taking out a business loan or a high-interest-rate credit card. The idea of either of those things terrified her. The business and the building it was in were their only assets. If anything happened, and the loan got defaulted on, they would not only be out of their primary source of income, her mom and sister would also lose their home.

Maybe that was dramatic and bordering on catastrophizing, but Juliette wasn't going to see them lose everything. Bad luck had a tendency to follow them around like a bad penny. Nothing was ever simple.

She'd been combing the internet, looking for a used stove, for several hours now. She'd tried restaurant supply companies, Craigslist, eBay, and an assortment of other sites she wasn't even certain were reputable. There was nothing within a four-hour radius. She'd have to go further afield.

On a sigh, she extended her search radius to five hundred miles. If they found something, she didn't know how they'd get it here. But that was a problem for Future Juliette. She didn't have the energy to waste on that until it was right in front of her.

Before she could click search, a knock sounded on her door. Derp scrambled up, staggering to answer with a cheerful bark. Juliette shoved back from her kitchen table, casting a quick glance around at the detritus of the night, noting the multiple empty mugs and crumb-strewn plates mixed in with the bank statements and spreadsheets. There was no help for the mess.

It was probably Mick, checking on her.

Or maybe not.

No matter what he'd said when he left last night, he might want to have some distance.

The idea of it made her heart hurt. It had only been a day, and she missed him. She knew she'd hurt him. But better to end things quickly now, than have them slowly die as all her responsibilities sucked her back in again. He deserved better than to come last in her life.

She tugged open the door, surprised to find her mother in the hall.

"Mom? What are you doing here?" She automatically fell back, making way so she could come inside.

"I need to talk to you."

Juliette watched her walk in, expert eyes checking for any signs of pain. But she seemed to be having a good day today. She wasn't struggling after climbing the steps to get here.

"Why don't you have a seat? I'll make some tea."

Sue Ellen's gaze swept over the mess on the table. She set down her purse and sank into one of the kitchen chairs. "Tea would be nice."

The last thing Juliette needed was more caffeine, so she chose a vanilla rooibos for herself and a specialty anti-inflammatory blend for her mother. Sue Ellen said nothing as she puttered around the kitchen, putting on water to boil and prepping the mugs. With each minute the silence dragged on, Juliette's tension ratcheted up.

What was her mother here to tell her? Were things even more dire than she imagined?

She stole a surreptitious glance at Sue Ellen, hoping to find some clue on her face. But her expression was inscrutable, some shade of the mask she wore to make them think everything was okay. Usually Juliette could see through it, but not today.

When she brought over the tea a few minutes later and sat, Sue Ellen nodded in thanks. "How goes the search?"

"Not great. But I have hope I'll find something." There simply wasn't another alternative.

Her mother looked entirely unperturbed as she sipped her tea. Why wasn't she more upset about this?

When Sue Ellen finally met her gaze, there was a steel in her eyes that Juliette wasn't accustomed to. "I want to start all of this by saying that I appreciate everything you have done for me. Truly. You have gone above and beyond from the time you were ten years old. I should never have let you take on so much."

"I don't mind."

"*I* mind. I let myself lean on you too hard, too much, and it's made you think that you don't have room for anything else. That stops now. I need you to recognize that I am a grown adult, and I can handle my business."

Struggling for patience, Juliette gripped her mug tighter. "Mom, I know you'd like to believe that. And I don't want to infantilize you, but look what's happened. You lost your temper with the health inspector and likely made this whole situation worse. Right now there is nothing coming in for income. If I don't find a replacement stove somewhere, there's not going to be any income coming. Beyond all that, you didn't even try to do the logical thing when Mr. Guthrie shut the gas off by coming here."

Frustration flickered over her mother's features. "Sweetheart, it's time I learned to depend on someone other than you. To that end, there is something I need to tell you."

Juliette braced herself. What was this about?

"Joe and I are dating."

Juliette blinked at her mother. "Who's Joe?"

Sue Ellen huffed a laugh. "Tiny."

"You and *Tiny?*" She didn't know what to say to that. "For how long?"

"This has been coming on slowly for a really long time. We've worked together for years. We've been friends for years.

He's been there." She reached out to lay her hand over Juliette's. "You've given up so much of yourself and your life to take care of me, of us. It's time you got to actually *have* a life. To do more of what you did this weekend with Mick."

An array of exactly what she'd done with Mick this weekend scrolled through her mind in high definition, and Juliette felt heat flood her cheeks.

Her mom's eyes twinkled in a way that suggested she at least suspected some of what had happened. "How is that going?"

That put an effective damper on her embarrassment. "It's not."

"Why not?" Sue Ellen demanded. "You two are perfect together, and he adores you."

Juliette adored him, too, but still she shook her head. "Maybe, but he deserves more than I can give him. So I ended it before he could."

Sue Ellen sighed and squeezed her hand. "Oh, honey. He's not your daddy. And he's not that weak-willed, selfish asshole you thankfully didn't marry back in college. He's stronger than both of them. As strong as you. And that's saying something."

Juliette had told herself that in North Carolina. She'd convinced herself he could handle her life. She'd even agreed that how much he could handle was his to decide. And the moment they'd gotten back, and she'd been slapped in the face with everything that had happened in her absence, she'd bailed rather than give him the benefit of the doubt. What kind of potential partner did that make her?

"Look, things are going to be changing," Sue Ellen announced. "Joe has asked us to move in for real. That frees up the apartment for us to rent, which brings in some extra income that will help offset the cost of a new stove."

Setting aside the subject of her mom having a relationship

she hadn't known anything about, Juliette latched onto the business side of things. "Over time, yes. But that doesn't help us in the short term."

"I know. But Mick's taking care of it."

Juliette's heart began to pound. "Mick's taking care of what?"

"He's fixing the stove we have. He's been down there all day."

"He what?"

"He called last night and offered to help. Between the two of them, he and Joe managed to narrow down the problem and source some parts. They should be about finished." Sue Ellen patted her cheek. "You should go down there and fix things."

Her mind spun. Was it really that simple? Had he really gone out on a limb for her family, even after she'd broken things off?

Of course he had. Because this was Mick. And that was the kind of man he was. It was one of the reasons she loved him.

God. She loved him. And she'd pushed him away.

Her throat went tight. "He must be so angry with me."

"Oh, honey, no. He's worried about you. He knows you're overwhelmed, and he just wanted to help. He's a good boy. I like him." She shoved back from the table and rose. "Now, head on over to Jade Palace to fix things."

As Juliette stood, Sue Ellen narrowed her eyes, skimming her from head to toe with an unmistakable mom look. "But maybe hop in the shower first."

NINE

Mick's eyes were gritty from lack of sleep. He and Tiny had spent half the night tearing the stove apart to figure out where the problem was. The older man had been more than a little alarmed by the prospect, but as Mick had pointed out, they needed a new stove, anyway. What did it hurt if they took this one apart to see if it could be fixed first?

They found the culprit somewhere around three in the morning. In addition to a deteriorating oven seal, one of the control valves was faulty. He'd scoured online sources, searching for replacement parts. The seal hadn't been a problem. There was one in Knoxville that he'd sent Tiny after. The valve was harder, but he'd been able to fashion a replacement in the machine shop at the garage. It wasn't an identical match, but Mick knew enough about making do that he'd been able to make it fit.

He tightened one last screw on the oven door and eased it closed.

"Perfect fit," Tiny observed.

"Better than it was, that's for sure. The only thing to do

now is call the gas company. We won't know for sure if this works until the gas is back on."

Mick stepped back, and they both stared at the reconstructed stove.

"I'm not sure the thing was this clean when we got it used years ago."

"It's not much different from an engine. No reason not to clean everything up while I was in there. It's just a good practice. You never know when something being gunked up can cause issues. If not now, then later."

"Think it'll work?"

Mick wiped his hands on a greasy rag. "Well, if it doesn't, it won't be for lack of effort on our part." He crossed the room to the industrial sink and began scrubbing the grease off his hands.

"I can't believe you did all this."

At the sound of Juliette's voice, Mick froze, his hands beneath the running water.

He hadn't expected her to show up. He'd hoped to have everything completely wrapped before he told her. He dared a quick glance toward where she stood in the doorway. She looked like she was about to cry. Or maybe run. There was a heavy dose of bafflement in there, too.

Tiny rubbed the back of his neck. "I'm... gonna go call the gas company. It's close to five, but a buddy of mine up there owes me a favor. You two should talk." With a significant look at both of them, the big man left them alone.

Mick wondered if she was willing to actually talk now, or if she'd do more telling.

He finished cleaning his hands and dried them before turning to face her. Juliette hadn't moved beyond the doorway. She stared at the stove, an unreadable expression on her face.

What did her being here mean? Had she changed her

mind? Would this be enough to prove to her that he could stick? That neither she nor her family was too much for him?

She was the one who'd ended things, so it was on her to make the next move. Hard as it was, Mick stayed quiet, waiting.

Finally, she lifted those big brown eyes to his. "Why did you do this?"

Mick shrugged. "Because I could. Because I wanted to help lighten your load. That's what I've always wanted."

Her face twisted. "You didn't have to do this. You didn't—"

Temper stirred beneath everything else. "Yes, I did." How could she question why he was here?

She rubbed at her temple. "It wasn't your responsibility."

Grandma, why didn't you tell me?

I didn't want to become your responsibility.

Grief from the memory made his voice a little sharper than he intended. "It wasn't yours, either. The fact is, I have a very useful skill set. One that you should have asked me to use."

"I never, ever want you to think I'm using you. That's... just, no."

Frustrated, he took a couple of steps toward her. "Asking for help isn't the same as taking advantage of someone or abusing the relationship. God, I wish you would use me. At least then I'd know that you actually trust me."

She flinched as if he'd struck her, and Mick felt like an absolute dick. But she didn't curl in on herself.

"I deserve that. You're right. I didn't trust you. I said that I would leave it up to you to decide how much you could handle. But in the end, it was me who couldn't handle it. The idea that we'd go on as we were and you'd eventually get sick of all of it... of me. I didn't know how to cope with the idea that someone else I love would walk away from me, so I cut things off before they even really got started."

Mick's heart stumbled. "You love me?"

Color tinged her cheeks. "You make it hard not to. You've been nothing but wonderful to me, basically always, and I haven't been fair to you."

Okay. Then maybe there was hope for them after all.

"Look, I don't blame you for any of it. I understand that what we came back to was a lot, and that you were upset. But I really need you to do me a favor."

"Anything."

He closed the distance between them and dared to touch her, chucking her under the chin. "Stop judging me by the shitty men who came before me. I'm not your ex. I'm not your dad."

"No," she whispered. "You're nothing like either of them." She swallowed hard, and when she spoke again, her voice was a little stronger. "I swear, I'm working on my crap. Unfortunately, I have a lot of it."

"Hey," he said, pointing to himself. "foster kid. I know all about baggage. Know what helps?"

"What?"

"Talking shit over with someone who gets it." He skimmed his hands over her shoulders and down her arms. "I get it, Juliette. Do you know *why* I'm so hell bound and determined to help?"

"No."

"My grandmother didn't tell me about the cancer. Not one word. She took it all on herself, until she just couldn't *do* anymore and the county took me away from her. I could have done something to make things better for her, if I'd known. We could have had more time. But she didn't tell me because she didn't want to be a burden."

Juliette's eyes went damp. "Oh, Mick."

"She would never have been a burden because I loved her. The people who matter never are. And whether we go back to being friends, or you're willing to rethink that something more, I'm still going to be here for you."

She stared up at him, eyes shimmering with tears. "You really are too good for this world, you know that?"

He grinned. "Ari says I'm a cinnamon roll hero."

Her lips quirked. "Sweet with little bite?"

"I mean, only if you ask nicely." As he watched her eyes heat, he added. "But you should know something first."

"What's that?"

"I love you, too. I've been ass over teakettle in love with you since about five minutes after you moved in next door. So maybe factor that into your decision."

Hope bloomed in her eyes. "I'd like to retract my earlier statement and pretend that last night's conversation didn't even happen."

Mick shook his head. "I can't do that. It did happen. And you remembering that it happened will hopefully keep it from happening again." He brushed the hair back from her face. "I need my girl to trust me, okay?"

Her hands snaked around his waist, and as her body came flush with his, Mick held in a cheer.

"Am I? Your girl?"

"I sure as hell hope so. Because I already told my family that I'll be bringing a plus three to dinner for Christmas day after tomorrow."

She blinked at him. "You want my family to come to Christmas dinner with yours?"

"Of course I do. And it makes sense, with the apartment out of commission. Although, I guess that should be a plus four, considering your mama and Tiny."

"You know about that?"

With a lift of his brow, he studied her face. "You didn't?"

"No. I just found out. I can't decide how I feel about it."

"Well, you can learn a lot about someone working all night on a tedious project with them. Here's what I can tell you: that man is head over heels in love with your mother. And he'd really like the chance to take care of her. It'd be great if you'd step back and let him."

Her chest rose and fell with a deep sigh. "I honestly never expected her to find happiness again. I'm thrilled if she has. And I swear I will try. I'll probably fail and have to be reminded. Frequently. But I truly just want her to be happy."

"I think she is. And for the record, she wants the same for you." He pulled her closer, linking his hands at the small of her back. "She thinks I'm good for you."

Juliette grinned. "She thinks you're a nice boy." She tipped her mouth up to brush his. "I think you're pretty great myself."

"Handy, that. And as soon as we're done here, I'd love to take you home and show you how great I really am."

She was laughing when he kissed her, and it was exactly what he'd needed.

JULIETTE PULLED up to the three-story Victorian. Lights and garland seemed to be draped from every railing of the wraparound porch, and a massive lit tree was framed in the front window. With its turret and wreaths, it looked like something out of a Hallmark movie.

The sight of all that holiday cheer reminded her of the Merry Falls Inn, where everything had changed for her. At the memory, something warm and squishy took up residence in her chest beside the faint anxiety over meeting Mick's entire family with hers in tow. She hadn't seen him since he'd left her bed this morning for his own family festivities.

She'd spent the day with her mom and sister at Tiny's

house. Though the gas had been restored to the building, Sue Ellen and Skylar had elected to stay put. They were moving in, after all. It had been weird, but nice, to have someone else included in their celebration. Now that she knew about their involvement, Juliette could only blame her myopic focus on problems for the fact that she hadn't noticed before. Tiny doted on Sue Ellen, and her mom seemed as fluttery as a teenage girl as they'd flirted their way through prepping food to bring tonight. They were happy. That did more to put Juliette at ease than anything else could have.

In the passenger seat, Sue Ellen leaned forward. "What a wonderful house."

It was a wonderful house. Juliette had never actually been here. Not in high school, when it had been nothing but a home. Not since Joan Reynolds' daughters had turned it into a profitable inn and spa. Now she tried to imagine what it was like for a much younger Mick to grow up here, surrounded by a family that wasn't blood-related.

As if summoned by her thoughts, the front door opened and he spilled out, face split with a welcoming smile. Knowing that Tiny had her mother, Juliette slid out of the car and went to meet her man. Just the idea of it had her grinning as he slid his arms around her and took her mouth with his. She sighed into the kiss, sliding her fingers into his hair. With a little hum of pleasure, she dropped back to her feet and smiled up at him. "I missed you today. Merry Christmas."

"Merry Christmas to you. Come on inside. Everyone's waiting." He glanced up at her family, extending the invitation to them as well.

Skylar and Tiny carried the covered dishes as they all made their way up the short steps to the porch and into the house.

A wall of noise greeted them. Christmas music underscored a babble of infinite conversations. It seemed there were people everywhere. Men, women, and so many children. A handful of people she knew from her school days or as patients, but so many others she didn't.

Someone let out an earsplitting whistle. "She's here!"

Everybody stopped and looked at Juliette.

That anxiety was back, tightening her chest. Instinctively, she crowded closer to Mick, feeling better as his arm wrapped around her.

"I'd like to point out that my girlfriend and her family are not zoo exhibits. So, if you would please remember to put on your company manners, I'd sure appreciate it."

Laughter followed Mick's announcement. Then people were coming forward, introducing themselves, even as they hijacked the food. They all got herded into the kitchen. It was a big room, with a massive farmhouse table that had two long benches on either side. The behemoth counter was groaning with more food than Juliette had ever seen in her life, and everything looked amazing.

Someone—she thought it might've been one of Mick's sisters—made room for the dumplings and vat of lo mein amid the other dishes. Someone let out another of those earsplitting whistles, and everybody quieted down.

A brunette that Juliette recognized as Pru Reynolds Bohannon, Mick's eldest sister, who was the official innkeeper here, raised her hands for attention. "Everybody, welcome to this year's Misfit Inn Christmas dinner. We have quite a few of the siblings in town, along with their significant others, and kids. We're thrilled y'all were willing to make the journey. On this most special holiday, it means so much to me, and to the rest of us, to have you here. Mom would have been delighted to see how the family has grown over the years. To see how well life has turned out for all her kids. So as we fall on this magnificent feast that has been assembled through the work of many hands, everybody raise a glass to Joan."

Her sister, Athena, the award-winning chef, stepped into the silence. "Okay, there are tables set up throughout the house. This is just like the old days. There are no assigned seats. It's first come first serve. We're gonna let the folks with the little ones go first, so they can get them settled and started before the rest of us do our best impression of ravening wolves. Everything is buffet style, so get in line. And most of all, enjoy."

As people began to shuffle about, Juliette let Mick pull her to a corner. He tugged her back against him, his arms around her waist as they waited for the crowd of parents to get through the line with their offspring. She enjoyed feeling his solid presence against her back.

"Good day?"

The warmth of his breath on her neck had her thinking about a whole host of ways to make it an even better night. But she managed to answer. "Yeah. You?"

"Good to catch up with sibs I haven't seen in a long time. But I'm looking forward to later."

"So, don't eat too much?" she murmured.

"Oh, no. That would be a crime with this spread. Eat as much as you want. Just know, the night ends with joint food comas and cuddling."

"I'm good with that."

When their turn in line came, Juliette knew in an instant that she'd have to make more than one trip because there was no way she could try a bite of everything on the first pass. All of it looked amazing. When she'd loaded her plate, she again took Mick's lead, following him through the house until they found a table with several empty seats.

She found herself seated across from Kendrick and Erin

Teague. Kendrick and Mick did some kind of complicated man-hug, then Mick dropped a kiss on Erin's cheek.

"How's the Baby Wildcat?"

"Hungry," Erin announced. Her eyes sparkled as they turned toward Juliette. "How was y'all's trip? Good?"

"It was great. I understand I have you to thank for the generous gift of the concert tickets."

Erin flashed a happy smile. "I'm just glad they didn't go to waste."

A Latina girl around Skylar's age snorted. "Oh, it worked. We don't have to be all circumspect now."

Brows drawn together, Juliette glanced at Mick in confusion. "What worked?"

It was his sister, Kennedy, who answered from the other end of the table. "What my very mouthy niece means to say is that we are a family of matchmakers. Everybody had a hand in your weekend."

"Including the Universe, it seems," Ari crowed. "Snowed in for days? I couldn't have planned it better myself. And I planned it pretty well."

"With my help." Skylar offered her hand for a high five.

As the two of them slapped palms, Juliette could only stare. "What do you mean, with your help?"

Skylar shrugged. "We totally set you up. You wouldn't get out of your own way."

Juliette had absolutely no idea what to say to any of this.

Mick fixed them all with a look. "There's a part of me that wants to be annoyed with all of you for interfering, but seeing that it worked out in my favor, I can hardly complain. So I'll just say thank you, and Merry Christmas."

Laughter rippled around the table.

When she just continued to sit, Mick nudged her shoulder

and whispered, "Just roll with it. It's better for your sanity that way."

Right. Just roll with the fact that her sister and a goodly chunk of Mick's family had conspired in a Machiavellian plot to get them together.

But she was happy. Maybe that was the only thing that mattered.

Conversation flew fast and furious, and Juliette wondered if this was what it had been like for Mick growing up in this house. There was so much obvious love among these people. So much support. And it became rapidly apparent that, through him, she and her family were now considered part of theirs.

As she sat surrounded by so many amazing people, Juliette decided that was a pretty awesome thing to be.

EPILOGUE

Mick scanned the produce selection at Garden of Eden and carefully added a couple of pints of locally grown blackberries to his cart, alongside the ingredients for a fresh herb and lemon risotto, some herb-butter chicken, and a summer peach and burrata salad. Juliette had all but swooned when they'd learned to make all of it at the cooking class they'd taken with Athena at The Misfit Kitchen last month, and he wanted to impress her tonight. If everything went his way, they'd be celebrating.

He made his way to the checkout. "Hey, Miss Ina."

The checker flashed him a smile. "Afternoon, Mick. Got big plans this weekend?"

"Date night tonight," Mick confirmed. "I'm cooking for my girl. She's got a special fondness for blackberry cobbler."

"Well, and who doesn't love a good cobbler? How's Juliette doing?"

"Thriving."

That was a lot easier for her to do now. Since Sue Ellen and Skylar had moved in with Tiny, they'd leased the apartment. That income had been put to good use, hiring additional staff for the restaurant, so Juliette was no longer working multiple jobs. She was still busy as hell with the mobile medical clinic, but she actually got downtime now to spend on things for herself. Usually, that meant him.

Life was good. And Mick hoped it would get even better.

It was nearing five by the time he made it back to his place and got started on dinner prep. He had the chicken marinating, the herbs chopped, the lemons zested, the peaches peeled, and he was just adding the honey balsamic reduction to the salad when Juliette let herself in the door.

"Hey. How was your day?"

She set her purse on the side table. "It was fine."

Mick gave the salad a toss and set it aside for the flavors to mingle before turning to brush her lips with a kiss. When she didn't linger, he pulled back, arching a brow. "What's up? Something wrong?"

"Not wrong, really. I've just been thinking."

His heart gave a hard bump as he wondered what she'd been thinking. But her manner was more distracted than upset, so he poured them both a glass of wine. "What about?"

Absently, she accepted the glass, closing her eyes at the first sip. "Mmm. Thanks. Well, for the past couple of years, my co-worker, Vicky—she's the primary nurse practitioner for the mobile medical clinic—has been trying to talk me into going back to nursing school to get my master's. I always shot the idea of it down because I had so much else on my plate."

"I sense a 'but' coming."

"But now things are better. She brought it up again today, and I'm actually thinking about it."

"Really?"

"Yeah. We need a clinic. The mobile medical clinic is certainly better than nothing. But we need a clinic in town that's always here. So I'm contemplating going back to school to finish my master's and being the one to open it."

"That's incredible! It would be an amazing addition to the community."

"I don't know for sure about opening a clinic. There's a lot of expense involved, and I don't know how all of it would work. But at the very least, I can finish my degree, and that opens up some more opportunities."

"That seems like a great way to handle it. The degree would be first, and then you can see where things fall."

"It would be another two years of training. Maybe three, depending on how much I can do while still working. I'll be hella busy with studying on top of my regular job."

"You're no stranger to busy."

She focused in on him, worry clear in those big brown eyes. "I'm just concerned that you'll feel neglected."

Ah, so this was the part that was stuck in her craw. He moved to cage her in against the counter. "No, I'm not going to feel neglected. You have a long-term goal that's for *you*, not everybody else."

"Yeah, but we'll probably see each other less. Because studying and class."

"Well, I actually have something I want to talk to you about that might help with that."

"Oh?" Pausing, she looked around at the in-progress dinner prep, clearly spotting the candles waiting to be lit and the neatly set table. Her lips quirked. "Mick Routledge, are you planning to seduce me tonight?"

He slid his arms around her, flashing an unapologetic grin. "Oh, unquestionably. I thought it might butter you up."

Her hands slid up his chest. "Butter me up for what?"

This wasn't how he'd intended to get into things. He'd

planned to ply her with good food and wine and the dessert he knew was her favorite. But he knew how sensitive she was to the idea that she wasn't putting enough effort into the relationship.

"I think we should move in together."

Her mouth didn't drop open in total shock, but her brows arched. "Really? That's a big step."

"Yeah, but it makes sense. We spend every night together, anyway. It would make more sense to pool our resources. Either you move in with me, I move in with you, or we find another place together that's bigger and better for both of us. That would help offset the expense of school and would allow you to maybe start saving some toward the expenses associated with opening a clinic."

She stared at him, her brain clearly working through the details. "You didn't know I was planning to do any of that when you set all of this up."

"No. Those just happen to be good practical reasons, and I know how much you value practicality. But the truth is, I love you, and I want to take the next step in our relationship. The question is, do you?"

He held his breath for her answer. But he didn't have to wait long for that smile he loved to bloom.

"There's nothing I'd like to do more." She rose to her toes, pausing with her lips just a breath from his. "Is anything currently cooking?"

"Not yet. Just marinating."

"Good. Then we can have dessert first."

"I haven't made the cobbler yet."

Juliette leaned back to grin at him. "That wasn't the dessert I was talking about."

"God, I love you." And they were both laughing as she towed him toward the bedroom.

Choose Your Next Romance

I HOPE you enjoyed this collection of Christmas hijinks! To nab the newsletter subscriber exclusive bonus epilogue, please go here: https://books.bookfunnel.com/a-little-lagniappe/ 64032dxfyg

If you're new to Ari's matchmaking shenanigans, feel free to start with *When You Got A Good Thing,* Book 1 in The Misfit Inn series, where she first appears. You can find her in basically every single book set in Eden's Ridge, which includes The Misfit Inn, Men of the Misfit Inn, and Rescue My Heart series. She also makes an appearance in *Single Dad in a Kilt,* Book 5 in the Kilted Hearts series.

Turn the page for a sneak peek of *Cowboy in a Kilt,* Book 1 in Kilted Hearts, in which a down on his luck Texas cowboy wins a Scottish barony in a high stakes Vegas poker game and finds out he's acquired a three-hundred-year-old marriage pact in the bargain!

A cowboy without a home

Robbed of the family ranch that should have been his legacy, Raleigh Beaumont is a man with no roots and no purpose. When a friend drags him to Vegas, he figures he's got nothing to lose. But after a hell of a lot of whiskey and a high stakes poker game with a beautiful stranger, he finds himself the alleged owner of a barony in Scotland.

An heiress with a crumbling heritage

When her brother's bride disappears just days before the wedding that's meant to save their ancestral home from the mad marriage pact that's held their family captive for generations, Kyla McKean believes they've been granted a reprieve. Until she finds out about the new, single—male—owner of Lochmara and knows she's next on the chopping block or ownership of both their estates revert to the crown.

A modern answer to a three-hundred-year-old problem.

Raleigh's lost his land once. He's not about to lose it again. Not even because of some lunatic pact made centuries before he was born. Kyla's desperate to save Ardinmuir. She agrees to marry him on one condition: They wed for one year to satisfy the pact, then get a quick and quiet divorce. There's no stipulation against it, and they'll both get what they want.

But this displaced Texan and his fiery bride are about to find so much more than they bargained for.

"It always rains the day a good man dies."

Raleigh Beaumont felt a smile tug the corner of his mouth, because the weather was bone dry. They'd been in a drought for the past few weeks. "Mama used to say that. She'd also say not to speak ill of the dead."

"Your daddy was probably the only thing your mama and I really disagreed on." Charlotte Vasquez came to lean beside him on the split-rail fence bordering the north pasture, propping one booted foot up as they both looked out over the rolling hills of the East Texas ranch that had been in his family for generations. "Luther Beaumont was a bastard, and we both know it."

"You're not wrong." One corner of his mouth quirking,

Raleigh glanced down at the tiny Latina woman, who barely came to the top of his shoulder.

When Raleigh's mama, Lily, had been diagnosed with stage-four cancer, it had been Charlotte who'd taken a leave of absence from her job as a high-powered executive and moved in to care for her—and by extension, Raleigh. His daddy hadn't stuck around to watch Lily's decline as illness stole her vitality and vivaciousness, leaving her only a shell of the woman she'd once been. Luther had thrown himself into keeping the ranch running smoothly. At the time, Raleigh had convinced himself his father was only outrunning the inevitable grief. That he was protecting the legacy he'd married into.

He'd learned better since.

"I mean, come on," Charlotte continued. "He moves that little hussy—" Said hussy being Twila, Luther's second wife, who was a bare seven years older than Raleigh himself. "—into the house when your mama's barely been six months in the ground? She only married him for his money, and he married her for the trophy." Her tone rang with bitter judgment, though it had been nearly fifteen years.

Raleigh stretched an arm across her shoulders, tugging her in for a hug. In the wake of Lily's death, Charlotte had convinced Luther to let her stay on as housekeeper, so she'd be around as a mother-figure to Raleigh because, God knew, Twila didn't have a maternal bone in her body. Back then, he hadn't understood what she'd given up for him, but at sixteen, that link to the mother he hadn't wanted to forget had saved Raleigh. And though he was well grown now, somehow, Charlotte had never left. He'd once asked her why, and she'd told him that losing his mother like that had shown her there were far more important things in life than breaking her back to climb a corporate ladder, and until she found another of them, she was staying planted near him.

"You didn't have to be here today. I'm a big boy. I can handle the reading of the will."

She squeezed him back, her head only coming to his shoulder. "Of course, I did. You need somebody here who's an ally."

They both turned to see a black Ford F-150 pulling up in the circular drive in front of the house.

"Looks like you weren't the only one with that idea," Raleigh murmured.

A familiar lanky figure climbed out of the truck and headed in their direction. Ezekiel Shaw was one of Raleigh's oldest and best friends. The one who'd as often been the instigator of mischief as the one to help him out of it.

Charlotte shot him a knowing smile. "Hey, Trouble."

Zeke grinned and pulled her in for a hug of his own. "Hey, Charlotte. When you gonna run away from this place and marry me?"

"I can't marry you. Who'd be around to keep this one on the straight and narrow once he takes over the ranch?"

He clutched his chest in dramatic fashion. "Breakin' my heart, woman."

"Somehow, I think you'll survive." But a twinkle in her rich chocolate eyes softened the dry retort.

Turning to Raleigh, Zeke hauled him in for a back-thumping hug. "You holding up?"

"Ready to get this show on the road. What're you doing out here?"

Zeke pulled a flask out of his pocket and offered it. "Figured I'd be around for moral support, just in case."

Raleigh waved away what he knew would be bourbon. "You think things won't go well with the reading of the will?"

He shrugged. "Got no reason to think one way or the other. I just know you and Twila don't exactly get on."

"She'll be out of my life soon enough." And thank God for

it. Raleigh was itching to truly take over the reins and begin implementing the plans for diversification and modernization that his father had rejected.

"From your mouth to God's ear," Charlotte muttered.

A whistle sounded behind them.

Hamp Browning, the family attorney, waved from the front porch. "Come on! It's time."

They strode toward the house, where Zeke dropped into one of the rocking chairs on the porch. "We'll see you on the other side."

Charlotte squeezed his shoulder once. "We'll be right out here."

Raleigh followed Hamp back to Luther's study. Kitted out in lots of wood and leather, the room still smelled of his daddy and the cigar he habitually allowed himself at the end of the day. He could just imagine the old man leaned back in the chair behind the massive desk set in front of the picture window that framed their spread. But it wasn't his seat anymore. After today, it would be Raleigh's.

Twila sat in one of the two chairs in front of the desk, looking like she'd come dressed for a board meeting instead of the reading of a will at home. She'd never fit in around here, with her city airs and high-heeled shoes. He didn't think he'd ever even seen her on a horse, and the only time she'd come out to the barn was to track down her husband. God forbid she risk stepping in something in her Feragucci shoes. Raleigh figured she'd be lighting out of here almost as soon as the reading was over. Back to Dallas, to her high-society friends.

He lowered himself into the other chair as Hamp circled around to the opposite side of the desk. The old man sat with a creak of springs and leather, running a hand down the tie that fell to the paunch overhanging his belt, then back up to smooth his big walrus mustache. Not for the first time, Raleigh thought he wouldn't look out of place as an extra in a western. Maybe in a leather vest at a poker table or behind the bar in an old saloon. The thought of it had his lips twitching into a smile. His mama would've appreciated the image. She had loved her westerns.

On a sigh, Hamp opened the folder he'd placed on the blotter. "Let's get to it, shall we?"

As the lawyer fell into the drone of legalese, reading the last will and testament of Luther Alexander Beaumont, Raleigh's gaze strayed past him to the window. Just a little while longer, then he'd finally be free to speak to the hands and their families, giving them the reassurance that nothing would change. They wouldn't lose their homes or jobs. His mind shifted to what needed to be his first orders of action. He'd had plenty of time to consider that, but he had to think about the season and what expenses the ranch would have coming up.

Abruptly, Raleigh realized Hamp and Twila were staring at him.

"I'm sorry. I zoned out there for a minute. Can you break it down into layman's terms?"

Hamp glanced at Twila, then back at him, his expression apologetic.

What the hell had he missed? Fighting not to curl his hands around the arms of the chair as a bad feeling set up like Quikrete in his gut, he waved at Hamp. "Go ahead; spit it out. I don't care about the money. I just want the ranch."

The old man winced. "Your father left everything to Twila."

That couldn't be right.

Shock was the only thing that kept his voice level. "I'm sorry. What?"

"All of it. He changed his will a few years ago. The stock, the land, the house. It all belongs to her now."

Raleigh exploded up, sending his chair skidding several feet back as he rounded on his father's wife. "This is fucking bullshit. This is my birthright. My mother's family's land. You have no right to it whatsoever. You don't want this place. You have no interest in running a ranch."

Unperturbed, she lifted her chin, somehow managing to look down her nose at him from where she stayed seated, her long legs crossed neatly in the slim pencil skirt. "You're right. I don't. Which is why I've already made arrangements to sell it."

The blood drained out of Raleigh's head. "Sell it? To who?"

She named a developer who'd been sniffing around for years with designs on turning their several thousand acres into cookie-cutter suburban houses.

As he let loose a string of profanity and began to pace, Twila examined her manicured nails. "You're welcome to try to beat the price." The figure she quoted was stratospheres above what Raleigh could afford.

When he said nothing, she flashed a smug little smile. "That's what I thought." She turned back to Hamp. "If that's all?"

At his short nod, she picked up her designer purse. "You have a week to clear out." Then she strode out of the room without a backward glance.

Raleigh scrubbed a hand over his head. "This can't be happening."

Hamp shoved up from the chair, looking about ten years older than he had when he'd sat down. "I'm sorry, son. There's nothing we can do."

"Can I take her to court? Contest the will?"

"You can try. But in my professional opinion, it's going to cost you more than you've got, and you're not going to come away with a ranch in the end. Luther was in his right mind when he changed his will. The bastard screwed you right and proper. There's no two ways about it."

The sucker punch of it had Raleigh swaying on his feet in a way the loss of his father had not. It threw him back to the devastation of his mother's death. He'd promised her he'd take care of the ranch. Take care of the people who worked there. Carry on their family legacy. And all of it had just been ripped away.

He didn't even remember leaving the room, not until he almost ran over Charlotte.

"Honey, what happened?"

Raleigh just shook his head and kept going. He needed out of the house, into the hot, humid air.

As soon as he hit the front porch, Zeke pushed up from the rocking chair he'd commandeered. "What the hell happened?"

"I got fucked, that's what happened. The old man left her everything. All of it. The entire ranch. My *mother's ranch.* She's selling it to fucking developers. It's gonna be a goddamn neighborhood here next year. My home is liable to be bulldozed or turned into some kind of clubhouse. Not to mention what the hell happens to all the hands and their families." Heart sinking, he scrubbed both hands over his face. "I promised them I'd look out for them, and there's not a damned thing I can do about it. She gave me a fucking week to get out."

His gaze caught on Charlotte's face. Her expression had turned carefully neutral, but she'd lost all color. He realized he wasn't the only one out of a home.

"Fuuuuuuck." Zeke drew the word out. "Man, I'm sorry. I don't even know what to tell you. I mean, I could—"

Raleigh held up a hand, knowing what he was about to suggest. "Not an option. Thank you, but no."

"Alright. Well, in that case, I'm thinking the best option is gonna be for you to get the hell out of town before you do something you're gonna regret."

Raleigh had no idea what he might do if he stayed and

wasn't much inclined to risk ending up behind bars. And yet. "I can't just leave. I need to break the news to the hands. Do what I can to help them find other placements. And I should pull together the family momentos before that bitch tosses them all." The idea of losing anything else of his family history made Raleigh sick.

"I've already done a lot of that, setting things aside for you over the years," Charlotte assured him. "It won't take long to pull together the rest. We should probably hurry before that harpy gets it in her head you don't have a right to them."

Zeke pulled out his phone. "I'll make the arrangements for boxes and storage."

As his friend stepped away, Raleigh took Charlotte by the shoulders. "I don't know where I'm gonna land with all this, but wherever it is, you'll have a place there. Always. You're family."

She cupped his cheek. "You're a good boy, Raleigh, and you grew into a fine man. Your mama would be proud. Now, let's go get to work."

***

"MAYBE NO ONE WILL NOTICE."

Kyla MacKean briefly shot her brother some side eye. "Aye. Right. No one will notice the six-foot-wide chunk of plaster that's crumbled off the wall." The remains of that plaster lay in a heap on the scarred hardwood floors she'd only just waxed and polished for the wedding reception set to be held here in a matter of days.

Connor shrugged with his usual insouciance. "It's a six-hundred-year-old castle. We'll say it's part of the ambiance."

"Be serious, Con. This is important. We can't afford for anything else to go wrong. Too much is riding on this weekend."

The reality of living in a centuries-old castle in the Highlands of Scotland was nowhere near as romantic as books and movies made it out to be. It was cold, drafty, and often wet. Parts of the castle were fully uninhabitable. The estimates they'd received from various contractors for truly weatherproofing the place were astronomical. Every single problem they discovered was usually a sign of a bigger, deeper issue that called for bigger, deeper pockets than they had. The truth was, they were land rich and house poor, and without a massive influx of cash, the home they both loved would fall to ruin. And while Scots did love their ruins, Kyla wasn't keen on living in one.

She had a plan. One that involved using her brother's wedding as an opportunity to show the world that Ardinmuir could be a premier wedding destination. People paid big money for that sort of thing. But not if the bloody walls of the great hall were falling down around their ears.

"Dinna fash yourself. It's stood for this long. It's no' gonna crash onto our heads this weekend."

"So say you."

He swung an arm around her shoulders and squeezed. "Aye, I do."

"Oh good. You've got your line down." She teased him out of long habit, but in truth, she was worried.

"That's right. Until I do my bit as the sacrificial groom, your bit hardly matters."

Kyla spun into him, clutching his shirt. "You're not thinking of backing out, are you?"

His beleaguered sigh didn't make her feel any better.

"No. I know my duty. I've had a lifetime to accept it. This wedding will happen, and the terms of the marriage pact will finally be satisfied."

Then the axe hovering over all their heads because of an

agreement made by ancestors who'd long since turned to dust would be gone, and they could get down to the serious business of actually saving the estate.

"I hope you know how much it means to me that you're doing this. I know Afton isn't who you'd have chosen."

"I'm certain I'm not her first choice, either. But it is what it is. We're friends. That's a far better basis than many have in arranged marriages."

Afton Lennox was the remaining heir to the barony of Lochmara, the neighboring estate. Her legacy fell under the same threat as their own, and Kyla could only thank God that she was willing to adhere to the terms of the pact. Then again, if she didn't, both their estates were forfeit to the Crown. Kyla would never stop cursing their ancestors for the addition of that little failsafe to the agreement meant to ensure the alliance between their families actually happened.

Knowing there was no changing their situation, she shook off the frustration. "We need to get someone out to look at it to make sure it's not going to get worse before the wedding. I don't want to have this place full of guests only to have plaster crashing down onto plates at the reception." Already feeling the beginnings of a headache, Kyla headed for the door. There was no getting mobile reception inside three- to four-foot-thick stone walls. "Maybe we can have a quick patch job done to get us through, then deal with the more permanent repair after."

It wasn't ideal, but she simply didn't have the bandwidth to deal with more disasters right now.

Connor followed her out. "I'm gonna go check in on Uncle Angus. The latest iteration of the wedding cake should be about ready."

"But the cake was decided on weeks ago! Why is he mucking around with it?"

"He reckons it'll be good practice for his audition for the

Great British Baking Show, and who am I to turn down more cake?"

Kyla closed her eyes and prayed for patience. She loved her great uncle and her brother, both, but sometimes dealing with them felt like wrangling a couple of cheerful puppies rather than grown adults. At least if Angus was baking, he wasn't out getting into some other sort of trouble. And, really, she wasn't going to turn down more cake, either, given how the day was shaping up.

It took longer than she wanted to get ahold of Theo Gordon, the contractor who'd done the most work on Ardinmuir. And longer still to convince him to come out today, after he finished up the job he was working the next village over. If a batch of Angus's jaffa cakes had been promised as a bribe, well, she'd run into Glenlaig to pick up ingredients herself, if she had to. It wasn't like they could finish setup until this was sorted, anyway.

Satisfied that she'd done all that could be done for the moment, Kyla made her way down to the kitchen, which was housed in the newer portion of the castle. New being relative, having been added on in the nineteenth century, when James MacKean, head of the family at the time, had been flush with cash from a shipping empire that later collapsed. But at least that part of the house had been comparatively modernized.

As she stepped into the kitchen, Angus straightened at the heavy wooden island, lifting his piping bag in triumph from a truly lovely confection of swirls and flowers.

Kyla sniffed the air and caught the tang of citrus. "If that's a lemon chiffon cake, I just might fall to my knees and weep with gratitude."

Angus's blue eyes twinkled. "Then ready your tissues, lass. But you'll have to wait until I take a picture for my blog."

"We have a deal. Although you may take that back when I

tell you that the only way I could get Theo out today to look at the wall in the great hall was to promise him a batch of your jaffa cakes."

One white brow winged up. "And what'll you trade *me* in this bargain?"

"My undying gratitude." Kyla slid her arm around him, and pressed a smacking kiss to his leathery cheek, feeling a bit of a pang as she realized he'd gotten a little more frail over the winter. Other than Connor, Uncle Angus was the last of her immediate family. When had he last gotten a checkup? She added that to the never-ending list in the back of her brain. Something to address after the wedding.

Connor snagged an Irn Bru from the avocado green refrigerator and kicked back against one of the long stone counters, smirking. "That disnae sound like much of a deal to me."

She pointed a finger at him in warning. "You stay out of this."

Angus considered. "You do the second round of dishes, and we have an agreement."

"Done."

As they shook on it, someone knocked on the door.

Connor pulled it open. "Malcolm! Welcome. Did you come to help with the setup for the reception, or did you hear a rumor that there's more cake?"

The brawny, fifty-something man stepped into the kitchen, kilt swinging, his thick-soled boots thumping on the hardwood floors. His hazel gaze slid over the cake on the island, but his expression didn't change. There were some in Glenlaig who believed Lochmara's estate manager to be surly, but Kyla knew the truth. He just preferred animals to people. In social settings, he tended to be a man of few words. Still, the prospect of cake usually would have garnered at least some interest.

A frisson of unease traveled down her spine as she registered the tension in his burly shoulders and jaw. "Is everything all right, Malcolm?"

"No." His throat worked. "Afton is gone."

The words hit Kyla like a well-aimed stone to the gut. "Gone? What do you mean she's gone? The wedding is in less than a week. She can't be gone."

"I found a note."

"Saying what?" Connor asked.

"That she's sorry."

"That's it?" Kyla knew her voice was edging into the realm of shrill, but couldn't seem to control it.

"That's it."

Like a puppet with cut strings, she dropped into a nearby chair. "You can't be telling me what I think you're telling me. If she's gone... If she doesn't go through with this wedding, we're all screwed. The Crown has been watching since we filed the paperwork for the marriage. We have to find her."

"Her car is still in the village. I tracked her that far before I came here. But she's gone. She could be anywhere."

"What about the police?" Angus asked.

"Since she left a note, we have no reason to get them involved. She's not a missing person since she left voluntarily." Malcolm spread his hands. "Unless you want to pour money into a private investigator to track her down..."

That was money they didn't have.

This was terrible. Disastrous.

Connor tunneled a hand through his mop of blond hair. "Maybe she'll come back."

Kyla shot a hard stare in his direction. "Are you willing to wait until the eleventh hour to see? I'm not. We all need to turn our efforts to tracking her down. She has to go down that aisle if I have to march her there in handcuffs myself."

Grab your copy of *Cowboy in a Kilt* today!

OTHER BOOKS BY KAIT NOLAN

A complete and up-to-date list of all my books can be found at https://kaitnolan.com.

Kilted Hearts
Small Town Contemporary Scottish Romance

- *Jilting The Kilt* (prequel)
- *Cowboy in a Kilt* (Raleigh and Kyla)
- *Grump in a Kilt* (Malcolm and Charlotte)
- *Playboy in a Kilt* (Connor and Sophie)
- *Protector in a Kilt* (Ewan and Isobel)
- *Single Dad in a Kilt* (Hamish and Afton)
- *Kilty Pleasures* (Jason and Skye)

Bad Boy Bakers
Small Town Military Romance

- *Rescued By a Bad Boy* (Brax and Mia prequel)

- *Mixed Up With a Marine* (Brax and Mia)
- *Wrapped Up with a Ranger* (Holt and Cayla)
- *Stirred Up by a SEAL* (Jonah and Rachel)
- *Hung Up on the Hacker* (Cash and Hadley)
- *Caught Up with the Captain* (Grey and Rebecca)

RESCUE MY HEART SERIES
SMALL TOWN MILITARY ROMANCE

- *Someone Like You* (Ivy and Harrison)
- *What I Like About You* (Laurel and Sebastian)
- *Bad Case of Loving You* (Paisley and Ty prequel)
  Included in *Made For Loving You* (Paisley and Ty)

THE MISFIT INN SERIES
SMALL TOWN FAMILY ROMANCE

- *When You Got A Good Thing* (Kennedy and Xander)
- *Til There Was You* (Misty and Denver)
- *Those Sweet Words* (Pru and Flynn)
- *Stay A Little Longer* (Athena and Logan)
- *Bring It On Home* (Maggie and Porter)
- *Come Away with Me* (Moses and Zuri)

MEN OF THE MISFIT INN
SMALL TOWN SOUTHERN ROMANCE

- *Let It Be Me* (Emerson and Caleb)
- *Our Kind of Love* (Abbey and Kyle)
- *Don't You Wanna Stay* (Deanna and Wyatt)

- *Until We Meet Again* (Samantha and Griffin prequel)
- *Come A Little Closer* (Samantha and Griffin)
- *Just Wanted You To Know* (Livia and Declan)

WISHFUL ROMANCE SERIES
SMALL TOWN SOUTHERN ROMANCE

- *Once Upon A Coffee* (Avery and Dillon)
- *To Get Me To You* (Cam and Norah)
- *Know Me Well* (Liam and Riley)
- *Be Careful, It's My Heart* (Brody and Tyler)
- *Just For This Moment* (Myles and Piper)
- *Wish I Might* (Reed and Cecily)
- *Turn My World Around* (Tucker and Corinne)
- *Dance Me A Dream* (Jace and Tara)
- *See You Again* (Trey and Sandy)
- *The Christmas Fountain* (Chad and Mary Alice)
- *You Were Meant For Me* (Mitch and Tess)
- *A Lot Like Christmas* (Ryan and Hannah)
- *Dancing Away With My Heart* (Zach and Lexi)

WISHING FOR A HERO SERIES (A WISHFUL SPINOFF SERIES)
SMALL TOWN ROMANTIC SUSPENSE

- *Make You Feel My Love* (Judd and Autumn)
- *Watch Over Me* (Nash and Rowan)
- *Can't Take My Eyes Off You* (Ethan and Miranda)
- *Burn For You* (Sean and Delaney)

MEET CUTE ROMANCE

SMALL TOWN SHORT ROMANCE

- *Once Upon A Snow Day*
- *Once Upon A New Year's Eve*
- *Once Upon An Heirloom*
- *Once Upon A Coffee*
- *Once Upon A Campfire*
- *Once Upon A Rescue*

SUMMER CAMP
CONTEMPORARY ROMANCE

- *Once Upon A Campfire*
- *Second Chance Summer*

ABOUT KAIT

Kait is a Mississippi native, who often swears like a sailor, calls everyone sugar, honey, or darlin', and can wield a bless your heart like a saber or a Snuggie, depending on requirements.

You can find more information on this *USA Today* best selling and RITA ® Award-winning author and her books on her website http://kaitnolan.com.

Do you need more small town sass and spark? Sign up for <u>her newsletter</u> to hear about new releases, book deals, and exclusive content!

www.ingramcontent.com/pod-product-compliance
Lightning Source LLC
Chambersburg PA
CBHW060556100726

47907CB00005B/1392